MYSTERY OF
THE DEAD SEA SCROLLS
REVEALED

SPENCER HAWKE

LONE MESA PUBLISHING

ACKNOWLEDGMENTS

Too many sources of great information have been used to chronicle this sometime fictional and sometime factual account of the Dead Sea Scrolls, not the least of which was Wikipedia. Internet search engines have provided a wealth of data, some conflicting with each other. All of the research used is of a public nature; if you feel differently, I beg your indulgence. I do not claim to be a historian, just an author with an over-active imagination. One source of great interest was Dead Sea Scrolls Deception by Michael Baigent and Eyewitnesstohistory.com

DISCOVERY AT QUMRAN

GOAT HERDER'S DESERT CAMP - 1946

Zayed screwed his eyes up tight, clenching his fist in anger, he could visualize his father's concerned face as he gave Zayed his best advice, "Don't ever camp at the water hole underneath Devil's pass in Qumran."

Zayed thought to himself in exasperation, "Why does my father always have to be right?"

When he drove his flock of goats through the mountain pass this afternoon all was quiet, he didn't hear a whisper from the pack of wild hyenas that his father said lived in the small cave above the pass.

It had been a very dry year; all the water holes he had tried bore no moisture. In desperation, he had driven his goats to Devil's pass. It always had the freshest, tastiest water. His flock began to smell the water before they entered the canyon, their pace quickened, their ears tensing, they brayed loudly to each other.

Zayed had tried to listen for any sound of the pack as he passed. He heard nothing, nor did he see any fresh tracks, so he decided to risk it, take his goats to the watering hole.

It wasn't until later that he heard the faint high pitched yelping of hyena cubs calling their parents, telling them to bring food. By then it was too late, night had descended, he had started his campfire and his flock had come in close to him, as if they smelled the danger.

A southerly breeze picked up, bringing the sound of excited pups sensing their parents' arrival. His flock gathered closer, it was now dark, even the light from the stars was partially hidden by the mountains. The wind gathered speed, as it squeezed through the pass it whistled, Zayed could hear a whistling scraping sound, it was eerie, so scary he decided to hold his orphan baby goat, Noora, close to his side. He nuzzled her face with his own. He was tired, but now he dared not close his eyes.

He added more wood to his fire. He was almost in a trancelike state, the sensation of holding his baby goat together with the warmth from the flames, put him into a shallow sleep. Even in his dozing state, there was no rest, he dreamed of his father, wagging his finger at him, "Zayed don't you ever forget what I have told you about Devil's pass, it has been the ruin of many a shepherd."

His dream was so realistic he awoke scared, with a slight sweat, he looked around to see if his father was there watching him. That was when he realized he was in real trouble, his hope for a quiet evening by the campfire, was dashed. He knew then that he was going to have to face his father, tell him that he had disobeyed his most ardent advice.

As he looked around the campfire he thought he saw the first sign that his life was going to change, he shuddered in fright. He wasn't sure, but for a moment he thought he saw two bright spots, like embers from his fire in the darkness. But these bright spots seemed to be less bright than embers, like looking into the soulless gates of hades.

Zayed shook in fright, he saw eyes, and they were moving, circling his camp. Then a second pair of eyes in the darkness…and those eyes did not belong to any of his goats.

He stood up, still hold tight to Noora. His fear was palpable now, he knew the mistake he had made; his father would never forgive him. But still the eyes circled his camp. He heard a wild yelp, followed by an evil laughing sound, as if the 'sentry' hyenas were calling the other members of the pack.

"Dinner time!" they seemed to bark out. His goats sensed it too as they huddled together so closely he could have walked over the herd without touching the ground. His flock looked around nervously, as if sensing that an attack by the desert's most feared predator was imminent.

Suddenly, the sounds of wild hyenas filled the air and the night was ripped apart with the screaming of goats and the "whooping" laugh of the savage beasts. Zayed could hear the hyenas barking and yapping at each other as they attacked the goat herd with a vengeance.

His goats began jumping over each other in an attempt to get away from their attackers. Zayed tried his best to keep the herd together, hoping to drive away the hyenas, but feared his efforts were wasted.

"Ha! Ha!" he screamed into the darkness, trying to herd his goats and waiving his shepherd's crook at the hyenas in a sad attempt to drive them away.

Over the next few minutes, the chaos and confusion continued as the goats were attacked and bitten. He thought he saw Noora's mother, the mother that had abandoned Noora, go down. She struggled wildly, bravely, but a second hyena charged in, ripped open her abdomen. The whooping laugh of the pack reached fever pitch, Zayed could watch no more. He knew he needed to do something, but what?

Zayed decided to make a run for it. He picked up his crook and took a whack at some of the hyenas; they just laughed at him. Those soulless eyes turning to look at him, while their jaws dripped with blood and entrails swung with their every movement.

He called out to the surviving members of his flock. "Shu, shu, shu!" he tried to bellow bravely, but his flock hardly noticed. He tried harder, shouting as loudly as he could, soon some of his charge started to follow; he increased his speed trying to keep the rest of the herd safe as they scrambled through the darkness.

As if matters could not be any worse, he felt the wind pick up. It now whistled loudly through the confines of the canyon walls. The wind began to feel heavy with moisture. Zayed knew what that meant; his years of living in the desert taught him about the heavy air at this time of year. He knew a sandstorm was about to pass through their area – but not just any sandstorm.

His father had also warned him about the mother of all sandstorms if they happened at this time of year. If he didn't find shelter soon, it could wipe out his remaining herd. He made a run for it, dropping Noora in the process and she brayed in fear. The herd was now running away from the sandstorm, the hyenas still following their prey, biting and chomping at the flesh of his goats whenever they got close enough.

Zayed was determined to save as many of his goats as he could and tried desperately to steer them toward a mountain pass. He moved side to side behind his flock, banging his stick on the rocks. Behind him, the hyenas slowed down, scared by the howling wind, their bellies full of goat meat.

"Shu, shu, shu, we must hurry!" Zayed shouted to the herd above the howling wind.

He quickly looked around, but could not see Noora. He feared he had lost her to the storm or the hyenas. Wiping a tear from his eye, he stopped suddenly, seeing something move by a nearby thick thorn bush. He ran quickly to see what it was and spotted Noora going into the hidden entrance of a cave. He followed her through the narrow passage, only wide enough for one person.

The entrance curved sharply, opening into a larger passageway. Zayed passed a large recess that had been cut into the upper side of the mountain and still housed enough large heavy rocks to close off the opening. Overhead, a thin furrow had been cut, as if designed so that someone might wedge in animal skins to close off the inhabitants from the night.

Zayed ushered the last of the remaining goats into the shelter and paused for a second to look to the south, watching the ominous dark clouds as they pushed the sandstorm forward.

Only a few moments later, he pulled his scarf up over his nose and mouth as the storm hit. The biting grains of sand batted against the cave entrance.

He turned to the dark interior of the cave and in the dim moonlight just barely visible through the entrance he could see the big, brown eyes of baby Noora.

"I am so happy I found you," he picked her up and headed a little deeper into the cave to get away from the biting sand, as what remained of his herd gathered around him. As he looked at the walls around him and the darkness that lay ahead, he wondered just what he had stumbled upon.

ARISE

BETHANY, JUDEA - 31 A.D.

"I worry he will not last the night." Mary leaned over the sickly white form of her brother Lazarus, mopping his sweaty brow with cold, wet rags. She looked to her sister, Martha.

"It's been over a week since we called for his friend, Jesus, to come and help us; I can't imagine what is taking him so long," she said.

Lazarus had been living with Mary and Martha in Bethany for some time. Now, he lay dying on a reed mat on their mud floor as they had tried to reduce his fever. Nothing seemed to work; he would not eat and was getting weaker and weaker by the hour as the fever retained its grip.

As evening cast its shadow over their small home, an old oil lamp, kept low to save money, showed the concerned faces of his sisters, weeping, still swabbing the sweat from his unconscious brow. Finally, the oil running low, they turned out the lamps and took their prayers into the darkness.

Martha awoke first the following morning, as the early light filtered into their room. She found her brother peaceful, head slightly to one side, still. No breath moved, and his body was cold.

"Mary, Mary, wake up! He's gone."

Mary looked at Lazarus then stood up chanting, "Blessed are you, Lord, our God, King of the universe, the True Judge."

At the same time, she was ripping her night shirt off in small pieces. Martha stood beside her, arm draped over her shoulders comforting her, all the time whispering in her ear to soothe her.

"It is all right, my sister," she said. "It is out of our hands now. We must prepare his body for a proper burial. We must go and get sanctified water to cleanse him."

Since Mary and Martha could not afford a casket, they wrapped Lazarus in a prayer shawl and a sheet and finally burial clothing, making his body ready to be taken to his tomb. Prayers and readings from the Torah were already being recited by friends outside the room.

The tomb stone to Lazarus' burial chamber would close him off from the living. As it was rolled back, Mary looked over to Martha, still choking up, "I wish Jesus had arrived in time to save our brother. I just don't understand what could have delayed him so long. Jesus loved Lazarus like his own brother."

Some days after Lazarus had been put to rest, young ragamuffins were out on the streets, playing. Whenever a traveler was spotted approaching town, it was a cause of great excitement and curiosity for the villagers, as not only did visitors bring fresh news, but quite often treats for the village young. As the youngsters spotted a stranger approaching, they ran to see who it was.

From afar, they recognized Jesus. By now everyone in town had heard about the sisters' disappointment that Jesus had not arrived in time to save Lazarus. Consequently, the children ran back into town shouting excitedly, "Jesus is coming! Jesus is coming! He has arrived!"

In no time, a large crowd assembled, since Jesus was already quite a celebrity. The villagers would have come to see him anyway, but with the added attraction of his absence when Lazarus was dying, people ran to see what would happen.

The ragamuffins led the crowd back out of town to greet Jesus, and as the people approached Jesus, he asked, "Where is Lazarus?"

The children could not restrain their excitement and shouted in unison, "He is dead! The village put him to rest four days ago!"

Jesus ignored them, continuing his walk into the village. As he reached the center, Mary and Martha approached, still grieving, the sorrow showing on their tear-stained faces and in their swollen eyes. They walked up to Jesus, everyone watching.

Mary tried to hide her feelings about his late arrival, "He's gone; you missed him. He was very ill; we couldn't save him."

Jesus looked at her with great empathy, "I am the resurrection and the life. He that believeth in me, though he were dead, yet shall he live. And whosoever liveth and believeth in me shall never die."

He looked at the surprised sisters, smiling and thinking that they had no idea what he planned. "Take me to his tomb!" he demanded loudly.

The crowd was even more surprised when Jesus ordered imperiously, after arriving at the tomb, "Roll back the stone covering the entrance."

He waited while some men came forward to roll back the stone covering the tomb. It had been placed in a little depression to keep it 'locked' in position, so it took quite an effort to start the stone rolling up the slight incline to flatter surface.

Eventually, they had the stone rolled back, and Jesus turned to the opened entrance. Bowing his head, he said a silent prayer, then out loud he said, "Lazarus, come forth!"

The crowd was too surprised to do anything. They probably thought Jesus mad. Everyone stared, amazed at his audacity, and all was quiet as they waited for whatever was going to happen next. Everyone except Jesus, of course, was surprised when a faint shuffling sound came from the cave, then more unidentifiable noises of movement.

The first people to see dropped to their knees in supplication, while those farther back in the crowd waited in anticipation. When they, too, were able to see, they fell to the ground in worship, as well. Lazarus was walking out, still wrapped in his grave clothes.

Martha and Mary looked at Lazarus, then at Jesus with total astonishment. They, too, dropped to their knees, bending over, their heads almost touching the ground as they gave thanks. Jesus walked off while they were all too awestruck to do or say anything other than pray.

SACRILEGE

JERUSALEM

"What is the meaning of this 'miracle'?" raged the High Priest.

Only the Sadducees had been absent from the raising of Lazarus. When they heard that Jesus was coming, they had stayed away. This rabbi, with his simple ways and "divine" message, was eroding the power base of the church and something must be done.

But they had heard the news. "If the villagers believe that this 'Jesus' is more powerful or the true Messiah, where will that leave us?" asked one priest.

"They will stop their tithes and offerings! The church will wither and die. Surely the Lord cannot endure this false prophet!' screamed another.

"The 'miraculous' raising of Lazarus from the dead is a complication. We are losing our influence among the people," the High Priest said, trying to calm the situation. "We cannot continue to have our popularity and power eroded by these 'miracles' of Jesus."

"What do you propose we do? My last assembly was almost empty, everybody wanted to go see Lazarus!" shouted another priest. "I cannot keep up my tithes to the council of priests if my believers are not tithing anymore!"

The Highest Priest of the meeting had had enough. There was nothing to be done immediately with this upstart Jesus, but there must be something done here and now.

"Lazarus is too popular; we must get rid of him," he said. "We need to have him killed, but it must look like an accident – perhaps a highway robbery gone awry – but it cannot be known to have come from us.

"If we keep track of his movements," he added, "then, when the time is right, we can let it be known there is a reward for his head."

REUNION AND A PLAN

LAZARUS' HOME IN BETHANY, JUDEA - 31 A.D.

"I can hardly believe my eyes, Lazarus! You are with us again. I have heard all types of stories about you. Is it true? Jesus raised you from the dead?"

Lazarus sat in his humble home with his good friend Barnabus. After his resurrection, he was well known throughout the land and those who did not personally witness Jesus' miracle at the tomb seemed to form a never-ending line of well-wishers. They all wanted to see a piece of the miracle for their selves – to see that Lazarus was, in fact, alive again.

But here was Barnabus – a dear friend who had waited until everyone else had gone. A Levite and a native of Cyprus, he had inherited land that he sold, and gave the proceeds to the church in Jerusalem. On his way back from his generous donation, he stopped in Bethany to visit Lazarus. As the crowd had dwindled, he entered the home of his old friend, and Lazarus greeted him with open arms.

"It is amazing – a miracle – but if what I hear is true, I may not live for long. The Sadducee high priests are so angry and jealous that they have put a price on my head," Lazarus said.

"Then we must get out of town! You are not safe in Judea. Where do you want to go?" Barnabus had already devoted his life to helping persecuted Jews, so his offer of aid was natural and immediate.

Lazarus had been dreaming often since his resurrection, unsure sometimes if what he saw was just a dream or a vision, but he did believe he had been saved for a purpose. He was ready to serve if he could just figure out what he was meant to do.

"I had a dream that I should go to Salamis, in your homeland," he told Barnabus. 'There we must teach Jesus' ways and build a temple for his followers."

Barnabus nodded excitedly. "If your life is in danger, we must go. Let's make for Seulecia. It's a Mediterranean port at the mouth of the Orontes River. From there, it is an easy day's sail to Salamis on the east coast of Cyprus."

Lazarus did not think it was going to be that easy to get out of Bethany, let alone make a long road trip to Seulecia with the Sadducee's spies everywhere.

"Barnabus, how are we going to get to Seulecia?" he asked. "Romans maintain some semblance of law and order in cities they occupy, but in the wilderness?" He let the question hang in the air.

"I think we can make it. If we dress as filthy, dirty, penniless vermin, they are sure to leave us alone. When we get to Mount Cassius, we will camp at the base of the mountain overlooking the harbor and await our opportunity to get a boat."

THE FIRST STEPS OF FATE

JERUSALEM

The Temple Scribe Gavrel wrapped the Torah in linen to protect it from prying eyes more than anything else as he carried it home.

As he walked home, he watched constantly over his shoulder, peering into every dark corner. The Romans had spies everywhere and the Roman occupation, as well all the taxes and assessments levied by both Caesar and the priests, were leaving many people destitute. Hunger and desperation caused many to betray confidences, friendships and family for a loaf of bread or a few shekels.

Gavrel hid the Torah and, after his evening prayers, tried to sleep, but he was restless. He tossed and turned on his mat, feeling as if someone was trying to tell him something. In his dream, he saw the peak of a mountain. At the base, two souls watched over a port in the distance. He recognized Seulecia then saw two men – Lazarus and Barnabus – camped under Mount Cassius.

A voice kept repeating, "Go to them. Lazarus will take Moses' Torah out of the Promised Land."

THE ROAD TO SEULECIA

Gavrel awoke the next morning after his restless night. He vividly remembered his dream, and, for some reason, he felt compunction to follow the vision. He decided to take the safer and more scenic route from Jerusalem, walking over to the Via Maris or Coastal Road.

Days into the journey, he was heartened to see Mount Cassius in the distance. Following the sweltering heat of the Coastal Road and the inland plains, it was a welcome sight to see the peak of Mount Cassius at about 4,000 feet above sea level in the middle of a dense coniferous Mediterranean forest.

After so long on the trail alone, he found he often spoke aloud to his donkey, Samuel, who simply trudged along seemingly unaware of their hardships.

"Do you smell the pine, Samuel?" he said now as the mountain came into view. "So sweet! And see how the silly goats are startled as we pass?

Even the locusts berate us for our intrusion, but they are nothing to be afraid of. See how easily you are startled!"

He led his team on, keeping a very tight rein on them, single file, through the well-worn, rocky game trails. Ravens flew erratically overhead, annoyed that their daily routine had been disturbed by his passage. They crossed the trail, gliding low and close, noisily letting Gavrel know they didn't approve of his presence.

"Be silent and be still, you foolish birds!" he bellowed at the offending ravens, as he traveled on through thick evergreen bushes into a rocky crevice flanked by tall conifer trees.

Although his demeanor seemed relaxed, he was secretly on full alert, looking for any sign of Lazarus and Barnabus. They didn't know he was coming to help them, so their reception might be frosty if he stumbled upon them unaware. The pair was fleeing from assassins sent by the High Priests, so they would be well hidden and scared.

Gavrel looked for any sign of human presence, a campsite or a fire. Suddenly, his keen senses picked up the faint odor of charcoal, but he kept going as if he had not noticed. When the smell was strong enough that he was sure, he decided the camp must be close by, so he stopped to make his own.

He was a careful man, more from his training in pankration than by natural inclination. He positioned himself so that the twisted branches of a thorn bush were directly to his back, making an ambush from the rear difficult. Next, he secured his animals, hobbled them and left them with plenty of food before sitting down to build a fire. There was plenty of dry kindling around, so the fire was started with little difficulty.

He was sitting on a log admiring his handy work when he felt the presence of someone approaching stealthily through the thorn bush.

"AAAAAAAAAAAGGGGHHHH!" Someone rushed at him from each side, one throwing rocks, the other with a knife drawn, both yelling like madmen, incomprehensible screams of adrenalin-fused fury.

Gavrel had no idea what they were shouting, but it sure got his attention. He didn't even think; his reaction was automatic and the result of years of training. His first move was to minimize his size, making himself as small a target as he could. He crouched low to the ground, catlike, assessing which attacker was the more immediate danger.

As rocks were landing all around him, he was a little off guard. He rose defensively with two hands on the ground for support and kicked out in a circular fashion to take the legs out from underneath the rock thrower. Gavrel didn't have time to notice, but the look of utter surprise on the man's face was priceless.

Next he turned his attention to the second intruder, who was further back. A moving target, he held the knife back ready to throw. Gavrel judged it well, and as the attacker's forearm started its forward motion, Gavrel moved lightning fast. He rolled away just as the knife landed in the log where moments earlier he had been sitting.

He grabbed the knife, and, turning to face his attacker, he pivoted preparing his arm to throw the knife back. The rock thrower, just recovering from his unceremonious dumping on the ground, saw what was about to happen. He screamed out, "Barnabus, he has your—"

Gavrel's reaction was instantaneous; his throwing arm stopped in mid-air. He had realized these two must be who he was seeking. He called out, "Lazarus, Barnabus, is that you?"

He could almost feel the surprise roll off the two frightened men, obviously flabbergasted to hear their names being called out by a man making camp close to their hideout. They were still very suspicious, but stopped their movements.

Gavrel continued to try to reassure them, "Lazarus, Barnabus, I am not a Sadducee spy; I have been sent to help you." He wiped the sweat from his brow. "Dear Lord be praised," he said in an earnest prayer. "I nearly killed you!"

Lazarus was not convinced yet, he wanted more information. "Who sent you to help us?"

"God."

Lazarus and Barnabus cautiously got up and looked at one another for guidance or direction. Barnabus decided to ask a question. "Where did you learn to fight like that? You could have easily killed us both."

Gavrel was trying to control his breathing, letting his adrenalin return to normal levels. "As a young recruit to scribe school in Jerusalem, I was ordered to take classes in the ancient fighting skill of pankration," he answered quietly. "I have been training for more than twenty years now."

Lazarus had heard of the ancient art, but Barnabus had not. Lazarus asked, "Isn't that what Hercules used in the first Olympic Games?"

"Yes, precisely," Gavrel replied.

Lazarus was still very uncertain. "But....Who are you?"

Gavrel was not too sure how to answer this question. He was here because an old stranger had set him on a path toward his destiny. That man had said he was the "teacher, "so he guessed he had better start using that name.

"I am the 'Teacher.'"

"The Teacher of Righteousness?"

"Yes."

Lazarus smiled now, as if that short name had explained everything. "I had a vision that I would meet you and you would explain my destiny, but I had nearly given up on you. Is He still looking out for us?"

This was all new to Gavrel, as well, but the answer became obvious to him. "Lazarus of the Four Days, why do you think His son brought you back from the dead four days after you had been in your burial chamber?"

Gavrel looked at Lazarus, waiting for an answer. After a slight pause, when he realized he was not going to get one, he continued, "You have a mission to fulfill. I have been sent to help you get to Cypress. The Lord has chosen you to take Moses' Torah to a safe place in Salamis. You and Barnabus will continue to Kition to build a place of worship.

"Your destiny," he continued, "is to take the Book of God's Holy Words to Kition and hide it in the vault that Barnabus will build in the Temple under the Moses seat."

FREEDOM IN A LEAKY ROWBOAT

MOUNT CASSIUS CAMP - EVENING

As darkness descended over Mount Cassius, Gavrel, Lazarus and Barnabus were seated around the campfire getting to know one another. Lazarus and Barnabus welcomed a share of Gavrel's ample provisions, as they were getting a bit low.

The last rays of sunlight fell beneath the horizon, and the cloudless sky began to fill with stars, first one or two more prominently, and then a symphony of magic appeared above them. The campfire was glowing on their faces when Gavrel decided it was time to get serious and see what plans the two friends had to get out of Seulecia.

To his surprise, Lazarus beat him to the punch, "Why do we need to move Moses' Torah? It has been stored for hundreds of years safely in Jerusalem."

"It has been foretold that Judea will be plundered once again. Jerusalem will fall, and for the second time, it will be laid utterly to waste, until there is no one left for the soldiers to kill or plunder."

Lazarus and Barnabus stared, incredulous; they shared looks of utter horror at the pure atrocity of anyone wanting to destroy all this history. Still, Lazarus was not convinced.

"Are you sure?" he asked, not wanting to believe it. "Who would do such a thing?"

"The Romans," Gavrel said sadly.

"But why?" Lazarus asked. He still couldn't believe that such cruelty existed.

"Rome will struggle for years to control the Jewish people and force them to obey the orders of their ruler. Instead, they will find only rebellion," Gavrel explained. "A general will be sent to quell the rebellion, but his eyes will be on the emperor's seat.

"Rome will call for all Jews to worship their Caesar as a god, but the Jewish people will refuse, clinging to the one true God and knowing it is a sacrilege to worship any other.

"The power-hungry general will turn his attention to the gold treasures of the Temple Mount," Gavrel continued, "and the destruction of all the Jews hold sacred – seeking to kill their spirit. Those who do not bow to the emperor will die."

There was total silence among the three new friends. "My destiny was foretold; it is to safeguard your passage to Cypress with the Torah," the young scribe said. "Then I must return to Jerusalem to prepare the way for the chosen one who will hide all of the remaining ancient writings from the Romans."

He looked at the moon. "Now it is time to make our sleeping arrangements."

Gavrel was feeling uneasy and decided it would be wise to hide their actual sleeping location away from the campfire. He would lay out false pallets to confuse any attackers and then select a place to lay their real sleeping mats very carefully. After much effort, he found a site that had thorn bushes on three sides, leaving only one approach for any thieves or murderers who might happen upon them.

He returned to the campfire, hitched two donkeys close by and laid out bedrolls full of cut branches. He took two other donkeys with him to the more secure location and hobbled and muzzled them after allowing them to graze for their dinner. Their evening prayers and studies complete, the three lay down close to Gavrel's precious cargo.

He warned his friends, "If you hear any disturbances while we sleep, stay put. I do not want to kill you by accident."

Later that night, Gavrel heard a commotion close to the campfire. He got up from his bedroll and crept over to the bushes overlooking the campfire to see two Roman deserters pummeling his fireside bedroll. He casually sidled closer, and as he got close enough to be able to confront them, he said facetiously, "Can I help you find something?"

The Romans looked up at Gavrel, shocked to see someone approaching them, then they looked at each other and back down at the bedroll. One of them gingerly toed back the blanket to see what was inside. When they discovered it was tree branches that they had been beating, the first Roman turned to his friend, "He tricked us."

The second Roman nodded his head in agreement, then in unison they moved menacingly closer to Gavrel, swords held high. As they got within striking distance, the thugs drew their swords back even further and higher to get more leverage. That was all Gavrel needed to see; he leapt into the air toward them, left leg coiled like a spring. As he came down, he released his left leg in a vicious kick to the first Roman's stomach. The man shot backward, gasping for air and bewildered.

The second Roman looked at his friend, then at Gavrel. He opened his mouth, full of black, rotten, broken teeth. He started to swing his sword, a vicious snarl on his face, shouting profanities, but before he could complete half his swing, Gavrel struck. He swung around to his right and launched his right hand open like a crab to grab his opponent's trachea between his thumb and four fingers, then squeezed. The thug dropped his sword and clawed at the clamp-like fingers, unable to breathe; he died and dropped to the ground.

Gavrel swiveled back to the first attacker, who was by now sitting up. He walked over to the man, put his knee into the thug's back and secured his right arm around the ruffian's neck. He pressed forward with his left arm, very angry and using too much pressure, "Why did you attack me? Who sent you?"

The Roman did not answer, and Gavrel continued the sideways and forward pressure, only to hear the thug's vertebrae crack. He released his grip too late.

Lazarus and Barnabus had heard the ruckus. Curious, they came up to see what was happening. "Is it safe for us to come out now?"

Gavrel did not want anyone to see the violence of the confrontation. "Go back to bed; we will talk in the morning."

He sat down, trying to get his adrenalin back to a normal level, and brewed some sweet tea. Then Gavrel tied a rope around the neck of each dead Roman and hitched them to a donkey. He pulled them a good distance from the camp and released the rope.

He had no sympathy for these unruly heathens, but for their souls he had compassion. After releasing their bodies a sufficient distance from their camp, he prayed for them. "May God rest your rotten souls, and I hope you provide a feast for the wild animals."

It was not a prayer he was proud of, Gavrel thought, but for these heathens it would do. After saying these few words, he moved slowly back to camp. If these ruffians had gotten this close to Lazarus and Barnabus, it meant the word was out and others would follow. The bounty on their heads must have been sufficient to even entice renegade Roman soldiers to hunt them.

Lazarus and Barnabus could not stay in these mountains another night; he had to get them to go down to the port to buy passage for Cypress in the morning. With those profound thoughts, Gavrel returned to his bedroll and tried to sleep. But it wasn't easy as he worried about his family, about Jerusalem, and about Temple Mount. He felt the weight of the world on his shoulders.

This was where his pankration training came to his aid. When confronted by multiple enemies at the same time, he had been taught to identify the immediate danger then move on to the next and so on, until all of his problems were resolved. It was only after he established the identity of his most immediate problem that he was able to relax enough to sleep.

Even when he did, every sound piercing his subconscious, he was still not totally comfortable with his surroundings; there could still be other assassins on their way. Instead, it was hyenas that disturbed his slumber. They had found his victims, their crazed whoop-whooping laugh echoing through the night. Other competing cats – leopards or cheetahs – contended for the free meal, snarling, growling and hissing to try to scare off the hyenas.

Gavrel took comfort in the ravenous predators, finally able to sink into a deep sleep – he knew these hungry beasts would alert him if any assassins tried to get close to his camp, disturbing their feast.

He woke early, strangely refreshed and at peace. It was an odd feeling considering the events of the previous night. Lazarus and Barnabus joined him around the fire as he tried rekindling it.

Lazarus couldn't restrain his curiosity. "What happened last night?" he asked.

"I suspect they were assassins sent by the Sadducee Priests. They died before they could talk."

Then deciding it was time to tell Lazarus and Barnabus his concerns, Gavrel added, "It is too dangerous for you to spend another night here; you must leave today."

With that decision made, they set about breaking camp, finishing their tea and extinguishing the fire. Gavrel confronted his two friends as they finished. "I must leave. Start your walk to Seulecia after lunch; I will be waiting."

Lazarus and Barnabus did as they were told. After a midday feast, provided by Gavrel, they left Mount Cassius for town. Lazarus confided in his friend, "I don't know about you, but I felt a lot safer when Gavrel was with us."

"Me, too, though he did say he would be waiting for us. Let's hope he is around if we need help."

The first sign of trouble came when some curious onlookers spotted them. Soon word spread and a large crowd gathered to see what would happen. The crowd followed closely behind, making both Lazarus and Barnabus very nervous with their loud chatter and whispered jests, but the pair continued their journey, feigning confidence with every step.

Halfway to their destination, Barnabus tried to reassure his friend. "They can't overtly kill you Lazarus; you are too popular. We need to continue down to the port. This is our best chance."

Lazarus held the Torah wrapped in linen close to his chest, holding it as if it were a prized possession. He made it very obvious that he treasured whatever it was he carried, and Barnabus whispered to his friend, "Lazarus, don't be so obvious with the Torah. You are clutching it to your chest as if it were a baby. Put it in your clothes bag."

He moved to do as Barnabus said, and they continued their walk. Soon they turned a corner and could see the jetty. The port had been rebuilt by the Romans into a strong stone causeway that led to many boats tied at anchor.

When they arrived at the jetty, they inquired about a boat to take them to Salimas, and paid for passage. They were led down to the jetty and were shocked to see a decrepit old row boat that was on its last legs waiting for them.

"Surely you don't mean for us to make the crossing in that wreck?" they queried the puppet harbor master from whom they had bought passage.

The crowd was becoming quite animated, some agreeing with Lazarus and Barnabus, muttering their support. Others, more mean spirited, guffawed and laughed at the pair's predicament. Lazarus and Barnabus looked at one another, and Barnabus said, "Don't you have another vessel that we could get passage on?"

The ringleader of the antagonists was a large, unkempt, toothless bully. He replied, "If you want to stay and wait for another boat, you can; might be a few days though."

Lazarus looked over at the leader of the conspirators, trying one more time, "This is what you want us to make the crossing in?"

The bully shouted out to the merriment of the onlookers, "Surely your friend Jesus will look over you on your voyage?" Animatedly, he looked around to see if the other spectators found it as funny as he did.

Lazarus and Barnabus realized their dire situation. There was no doubt these people knew who they were, and it was either paddle and perhaps drown or stay here and wait for the Sadducee assassins to come.

They walked over to the boat and sat down. Barnabus, being the stronger of the two, manned the oars, while Lazarus started bailing out water with his hands.

Lazarus whispered to his friend, "What are we going to do? The sea water will destroy the Torah."

"We can't go back. Tie the clothes bag on your back and start bailing water. We might have to row to the other side of the harbor and steal another, better boat," Barnabus said. "If we can make it to the fog bank, perhaps they won't see us. And pray that Gavrel is watching."

The crowd watched as the boat slowly moved off into the gathering evening mist of the Mediterranean. Barnabus rowed like crazy, but made little progress, while Lazarus bailed as quickly as he could, but the water continued to rise.

The crowd was noisy, enjoying the spectacle, some laughing loudly. Ever so slowly, they inched their way toward the cloud bank, and after what seemed like an eternity to them, the row boat grudgingly entered the fog. A rather large wave rocked the boat as the mist in front of the row boat darkened. To their utter surprise, painfully slowly, a ship materialized out of the fog.

A square-rigged cargo ship pulled in its sails, gliding up alongside the leaky row boat. Standing on the bow of the ship was Gavrel, majestic, beard and long braids blowing back from his sunburned face. He waved his new friends over, and Lazarus, relieved to be able to keep the Torah dry, threw it to Gavrel then abandoned the row boat to scamper up to the cargo ship.

Gavrel turned to the captain, "Set sail for Cypress, Captain."

He turned to Lazarus and Barnabus who were seated on the deck trying to get their wind back. "You are in for a treat; a crossing from Seulecia to Cypress on a square-rigged brig, captained by a master of his craft, is an experience to treasure."

Lazarus smiled like an alley cat. "You are full of surprises!"

The misty evening of Seulecia gave way to a seductive breeze from the southeast, blowing through everyone's hair and lightening the mood of all. The breeze was clearing the mist as well.

"Gavrel, do you smell the faint citrusy freshness from the groves along the coast?" Barnabus asked. "Must be a good omen."

The scented wind bristled through the captain's whiskers as he stood face to the wind, "First Mate, raise the yard on the main mast and make way."

The captain turned the brig to front the breeze. The sails filled, and the brig creaked as it gathered speed. The sun was coming up over the mountains.

In the distance to the northwest, the captain pointed out a motionless cloud bank. "Cypress."

Before long, a troop of dolphins took up riding the bow waves, swimming up from the back, riding the crest and then flipping over and speeding up to repeat the process on the other side. The whole time, they made a high-pitched "e-e-e," or clacking noise like castanets, screeching in joy.

As Seulecia disappeared from view, Gavrel called Lazarus over to the bow of the brig to sit with him and share a snack of olives, cheese and figs. "Lazarus, have you given much thought to your mission?"

Lazarus thought for a moment then answered, "For some time, I have had this same dream. In this vision, I must follow Jesus and teach his words. I feel that I am being led in a direction, though I don't always know where I am going. It is the strangest feeling."

Gavrel nodded his understanding. "Lazarus, you must not worry so; God will guide you when the time is right."

Lazarus finally smiled. "I wish I could have seen the faces of the Sadducees spies when you appeared out of the mist to rescue us."

"Yes, you were too busy climbing on board to notice, but those traitors were as mad and frustrated as could be. Something tells me that they haven't given up yet on the reward."

Then he added, trying to make light of the situation, "You should have asked for a refund!

"When we get to Salimas, you will be met by the owner of this boat – a Joshua Guggenheim of the Guggenheim Trading House," Gavrel said. "He or his family will meet you at the port to take care of you. He will guard the Torah for you.

"You must minister to his family and congregation. He will provide you and Barnabus with letters of introduction to other synagogues for your journey to Kition."

Both of Gavrel's new friends were surprised by this. "Are you not coming with us?"

"This brig is taking a cargo of copper and silver to Tyre after docking at Salimas. I do not want to go back through Seulecia. Landing at Tyre will save many days of travel," he said. "I must return to Jerusalem. I have much work to do."

BLACK BEDOUIN

NEGEV DESERT - 44 A.D.

"Shhhh …. They said," just loud enough for him to hear. "The black Bedouin is watching."

Hilal was at his work station by his parents' tent. He looked over at the other village children with envy as they played and he worked. Some of the children saw him watching and began to bully him.

Hilal tried to ignore them, as they whispered loud enough to be heard, "I hear his family even eats wild dogs."

Then another said, "What do you expect from a black Bedouin from the Sudan? I hear they even eat their dead."

He wiped the tears forming in his eyes. Ignoring the taunts, he continued to soak his father's goat skins in a lime solution then scrape both sides with a knife and rinse them with water. Those with minimum flaws, he carefully laid to one side to be made into parchment.

Hilal's father supported the family through his goat herd. A strict disciplinarian, his father tended his flock while his wife looked after the home and his son worked with goat skins. Since his father kept him busy in the family business, Hilal never had time to run wild with the other boys in the village of Wadi Zuballa.

When he did not react to their taunts, the bullies became bored and moved away to find more interesting prey. At last, Hilal finished the remaining skins on which he had been working. He wanted them ready so he could take them to the village market.

He saw his mother approaching, shouting his name, as she tried to find him. "Hello, Mother!" he called to her. "I am going to take some of my skins to the market. The buyers are in town. I'll be back before nightfall."

She looked lovingly at him. "Be back by dark, my son."

Hilal had worked hard for as long as he could remember and was now a boy with strong muscles, an athletic build and a cherubic face with straight white teeth that shined out from his winning smile, highlighting his button nose. His dark brown eyes glowed with happiness – that is, unless he was being harassed by the village vagabonds.

He selected his finest skins, putting them in a pile to take to the market.

When he was satisfied with his selection, he began the trek across his village.

As he turned a corner, he could see the market in the distance. It looked like it was opening. The hot afternoon sun had started to go down, making the temperature more bearable, Hilal skipped along happily thinking of all the skins he could sell. Suddenly, the bullies who had moved on from his work area earlier in the day reappeared between him and his goal.

"The Black Bedouin!" he heard one boy shout. "Who let you out of your tent, dog-eater?"

The leader of this band of young bullies was Jude. In Arabic, the name means kindness and goodness, but in this case, it simply did not fit. His parents let him run wild, his curly brown hair long and unkempt. When his locks were swept away from his face, it revealed one eye that had no warmth, the other permanently closed and swollen. His hawk-like nose added to his sinister looks.

Hilal clutched his skins tighter, knowing these belligerent children would make his passage painful. He saw Jude give the nod – no mercy, make no way for the Black Bedouin.

But Hilal was determined; he gritted his teeth and pressed forward, trying to push his way through. The children formed a blockade, lining up side by side, and as he charged ahead, the bullies circled him, pushing him and his skins from one side of the circle to the other.

Hilal could not defend himself because he held on to his prized parchments with determination. They elbowed him, taunting him, shouting at him, "Here is the Sudan boy again!"

He pushed on resolute that he would pass, trying to break free. Some of the bullies tried to grab his skins, but he twisted and turned, avoiding their outstretched hands.

The gang continued to verbally abuse him, "These aren't real parchment; these are hyena skins! I bet his family eats wild dogs."

They looked from one to another for affirmation, gaining courage from being part of the group. "That's what they do in the Sudan!"

Hilal struggled with the gang, as one punched him, another tried to steal his skins while he was off balance. Most of the skins fell to the ground, and Hilal tried desperately to pick them up, the dust from all the trampling feet making his quest all the more painful. The children kept pushing him down, until eventually the bullies succeeded in making him drop all of his skins. He went to his knees trying to recover them, coughing and spluttering in the thickening dust.

As he picked up his goods, he sobbed, but still managed to defend his family's honor, "These aren't hyena skins; these are goat skins! My family doesn't eat dog meat; we are civilized Bedouins and not from the Sudan."

Tears formed again in Hilal's eyes as he struggled with the bullies. They pushed him some more, and the skins on the ground were stamped on, his other skins, ripped from his hands. Again he fell to his hands and knees, but managed to recover all of his skins. In the distance, he heard the buyers haggling over skin prices.

One buyer said loudly, "That is too much! These are not the best quality; I only want the best."

Hilal, still on his knees, gathered up all of his dusty skins and scrambled off under the legs of the bullies. Next he confronted the crowd in front of the buyers, startled as Hilal pushed his way through under their feet. He tried to get up with his skins, but the older people in line and those circling the edge of the buyers elbowed him back to the ground, making it difficult for the boy to get in front of a trader.

Eventually he arrived close to the buyers, still on all fours. He tried to shake the dust off his skins. With one final effort, he made a mad dash to get in front of a scribe buyer. He was desperate and still on his knees, but he succeeded.

He lifted up some skins, "Here! Please, look at the quality of my skins," he begged.

The scribe buyer, seeing the tormented, dusty face, took pity on him. "Show me your best."

Hilal passed his proudest skin to the scribe. "Here, look, I cured this myself."

The scribe pulled out a quill and started writing on the parchment. Hilal tried but could not read the strange shapes the buyer was making. He continued to stare, fascinated.

Finally, the scribe asked Hilal, "How much do you want for the skins?"

"I need enough money to travel to Jerusalem, so I can learn to write like you."

This was a first for the scribe, mystified, he asked, "Why do you want to learn to write?"

Hilal was gasping for air, talking quickly, "All the village children taunt me and my family, calling us 'Black Bedouin' and telling lies that we eat dog meat. I want to show them that I am a proud Bedouin and also a scribe. Then perhaps I can join the Council of Elders of our tribe. I will make sure my children are not bullied by bigger boys."

The scribe buyer was sympathetic, he told Hilal, "Go to the Holy City, and ask for me, my name is Hillel. I have the best school. What is your name?"

"Hilal."

The look on the scribe's face was as if he had seen a ghost. Hilal noticed but didn't say anything. It took the scribe a moment to regain his composure. When he did, he said in a very serious manner, looking Hilal square in the eyes, "Hilal, you say?" Hilal only nodded.

"I will remember you, Hilal."

The scribe turned, picked up his small stool and bag and left the market. How strange, thought Hilal, though he was secretly overjoyed he had made friends with a scribe in Jerusalem.

FOLLOW YOUR STARS

The day finally arrived for which Hilal had so long been planning. He had been at work since early that morning, and he was tired.

As the sun descended to the west horizon, the light was no longer strong enough for Hilal to see his work. He put away his tools and finished stretching and securing the skins he had been preparing, then looked up to see his mother approaching their home.

Hilal walked into the family tent to speak to his mother, blurting out a little quicker than he wanted, since he was nervous, "Mother, I must go find father; I have something very important to discuss with him."

Every night for the past month, Hilal lay awake, thinking of his dream to learn how to read and write so he, too, could become the Chief of his Tribe on the Council of Elders. During the day, he planned the best way to approach his father. Even at his young age, he knew that if he waited until his father was home to talk to him, his mother, who was so over-protective, would talk his father out of letting him go, so he had to talk to his father alone.

His mother was somewhat surprised by his uncharacteristic outburst, "Hilal, what can possibly be so important that you cannot wait for your father to come back?"

"Mother, I have to go see him now; it is very important."

He was right in his assessment; his mother was very protective, and it looked like she was going to put her foot down.

"Hilal," she responded, "It is far too dangerous for you to go by yourself. Your father is four hours' walk from here; you can't possibly go now, besides it is getting late."

He was prepared for this, knowing his mother would not give in easily.

"Mother," he replied, "I have been traveling these trails alone since I was little, I'll be fine."

His mother thought that pretty funny. She still thought of him as her little boy, but she was adamant, "No, it is too dangerous; that is final. Go rest up, and I will call you when food is ready." She did not want to hear any more argument.

"Mother, you do not understand," Hilal responded sulkily.

He gave up. His mother was not going to let him go. He retreated to his sleeping quarters to carry out his plan as his mother went to prepare food for their evening meal.

Later, when darkness descended, she called him to come eat. Hearing no answer, she called again, "Hilal, time to eat, clean your hands." No response.

"Hilal, stop ignoring me, it's time to eat," she tried again.

Exasperated, she walked to the sleeping quarters, only to find him gone, a slight opening forced in the goat hair wall. Eyes wide in fright, terrified for her son, she turned around and ran out looking for her brother.

HILAL'S SLEEPING QUARTERS - EARLIER THAT EVENING

Hilal had made up his mind. He forced a hole in the goat hair tent big enough to let him through and crawled out, leaving his home. Determined, he stealthily started his trek east.

Initially, he stood strong with the conviction of his decision, strutting arrogantly into the desert. He did not even look behind him. But as darkness descended and the enormity of his decision became reality, his pace shortened with uncertainty.

He began to jump at shadows and to talk to himself angrily. "What are you afraid of, Hilal? You are skittering through the desert like a little boy!"

He saw his shadow in front of him and noted it was already longer than he was tall. Suddenly, he realized it would soon be very dark and would be awfully scary until the moon came up.

After a few more minutes over rocky, uneven terrain, he approached a wadi. He descended into the dry river bed and sneaked a look over his shoulder. He could only just see the outline of the village camp.

Over a lump in his throat, he squeaked, "Be a man, Hilal. You have crossed this wadi a thousand times!"

He continued across the wadi, watching intently for any slithering tracks that could foretell of hidden danger where critters may be lurking, waiting on the careless to approach.

He finally climbed the east side of the wadi. It was too dark to see his village now, and the emotions running through his mind were overwhelming, doubt increasingly creeping into his subconscious. He continued east, looking constantly to see if he could see the Big Dipper in the sky to confirm the direction he was traveling.

Hilal tried closing his eyes, tuning his ears to the sounds of the night. A faint breeze dislodged tiny grains of sand, forcing the dry rock fragments to tumble head over heels, creating a faint, eerie scraping sound.

As the moonlight grew stronger, it exposed luminescent outlines of scorpions scampering across the dunes.

Locusts also jumped as he passed, startled – sometimes, skipping toward his face and scaring him even more, causing him to doubt with greater intensity his crusade to talk to his father. But he kept going, wiping the tears from his eyes.

HILAL'S FAMILY HOME IN WADI ZUBALLA

"Thanoon, please help..... My little boy has run away! I think he has gone to his father's camp."

When Hilal's mother discovered him missing, she ran across the village to her brother's tent, bursting through the opening, babbling to her brother Thanoon in a total panic.

Thanoon was relaxing, stretched out on pillows, enjoying his rest. He had just come back from one of his long trips to Aqaba.

Not easily moved from his comfortable slumber, he asked, "Why would he do that?"

"He asked me earlier if he could leave to go see his father tonight. I, of course, said no. But he is just like his father; he doesn't listen to a word I say."

Thanoon had still not moved from his pillows on the floor. He frowned thoughtfully, "I think I know why. Some village children have been harassing him, trying to humiliate him whenever he is away from home."

He sprang to his feet in sudden anger. "That village mongrel, Jude, has been encouraging his gang to call Hilal all sorts of names and hurt him whenever they can. In fact, I am going to talk to him and his family right now."

Hilal's mother was grief stricken, "Brother, oh please, not now. Talk to them later. Can you go now, follow Hilal; keep my baby safe?"

Thanoon walked toward the tent opening. "I will follow him and keep him safe."

He turned to his sister, hugged her, and left his home in a hurry.

Hilal's mother watched her brother take off after her son. He was moving fast, and was soon lost to view.

THE NEGEV DESERT

Thanoon followed the same path Hilal had taken. The older man had been traveling the desert since his childhood, and he was very proud of his skill at using the stars at night or his hard-earned intuition during the day for navigation. After some time, he spotted Hilal, the boy's black robe casting an ominous shape against the brightening moonlight.

Thanoon watched the boy silently; he even got close enough to hear some muffled sobs. He saw Hilal wipe away his tears, but Thanoon stayed behind, comforted that the child was safe and no bullies from the village were following him.

"Ah, my sister, I know that you want your child home in your arms even kicking and screaming," Thanoon spoke aloud to his camel, which oddly seemed to be listening to every word. "But a boy must sometimes be allowed to grow up, make decisions and learn from them.

"We will follow, and we will watch," he said, patting the camel's strong neck. "We will keep him safe as he learns this lesson."

HILAL'S FATHER'S GOAT HERD

During the day, goats tend to forage and wander independently. At night, they prefer to gather in much closer proximity for safety. Hilal spotted his father's campfire from far away; as he got closer, he could see his father stand, looking for the cause of the sudden uneasiness of his herd. Hilal saw his objective in sight and lengthened his stride, more certain now. As he approached, his father recognized him.

Hilal was so relieved to find his father, he yelled out in relief, "Greetings, my father!" He quickened his pace even more to go hug the waiting man.

Hilal's father was also surprised to see his son traveling alone, "Peace be with you, my son."

The Bedouin tradition of hospitality would not allow Hilal to tell his father the reason for his visit until they had exchanged pleasantries over coffee. Likewise, his father, although curious, could not ask Hilal the reason for his unexpected appearance.

His father started to make coffee. He offered his son dates and goat cheese. He crushed some green coffee beans in a brass mortar, adding a little cardamom. He added some boiling water that was steaming over a brush wood fire. After some minutes, he poured the steaming liquid from the long-beaked brass pot into small, porcelain, egg-sized cups and handed one to Hilal. They savored the gritty brew together in peace, but Hilal could withhold his news no longer.

Bursting with excitement, he said, "Father, I have something of great importance to discuss with you."

Father and son looked at each other across the campfire. A long silence followed as Hilal's father waited.

"Father, I want your permission to go to the Holy City to learn the ways of the scribes. I want to learn from them so I can also become versed and respected; perhaps I will be able to join the Council of Elders. Then no one will call us Black Bedouins again."

Hilal's father maintained his silence, waiting for Hilal to continue. That silence was only interrupted by goats braying – the sound like small children crying – and the crackling fire.

"Father, I know this must be a disappointment to you, but I feel this is a path I must follow. I would like your blessing."

His father rose, looked up at the stars, and the fire lit his face, showing a look of sadness and yet understanding. "My son, do you see the stars above us?"

Hilal was surprised at the question, expecting something a little more profound. "Yes, Father, of course."

"My son, although the Bedouin have used the stars for centuries to guide us, they lead us all in different directions. We must all follow our stars." There was silence between them for a few minutes, and Hilal knew instinctively not to interrupt; he simply waited.

"I am not disappointed," his father said. "Rather, I am very proud that you have come to me to seek my blessing. But you are too young. I cannot give you my permission, perhaps when you are older..."

Hilal had feared this would be his father's answer. The emotional torment he had endured these last weeks anticipating this meeting was too much; he broke down in tears, unable to hold back his grief.

"But Father, by then it will be too late. I won't be able to learn to read and write. When I am married, the village boys will bully my children, call them names, as they do with me."

His father's gentle, loving demeanor changed abruptly; he had no idea what his son was talking about. "I think you had better tell me what has been going on."

Hilal tried to tell his father about Jude and his gang of bullies. "The village boys always call me names. They say we are Black Bedouins, second-class members of our tribe. They say you eat dogs and that we should not be a part of this Bedouin family. They say because we are from the Sudan that we are second-rate and whenever I leave home to go to market they try to follow me, harass me, steal our skins to throw them to the ground, stamp on them."

Hilal had not seen his father so angry in many moons. He rose from his seat around the fire, his aggravation so intense that he couldn't keep still, and paced forward and backwards, almost shouting back at his son. "They do that? The vermin try to bully you, just because we are from the Sudan?"

"Yes, Father, look...."

Hilal lifted his robe up from his ankles to show his father his scraped and bloody knees, then his scuffed elbows and lastly the bruises on his chest.

His father's anger raised another notch, even more furious, he paced, thinking, finally coming to a decision. His mind made up, he turned to his son, "Those vermin! I am going to stay closer to our village from now on. I will work on being asked to join the Council of Elders. When you come back from your studies, you should then be able to be elected the Chief Elder of the Council."

Looking down at his son proudly, he added, "We will show them – you and me together!"

Hilal's father was still pacing, rubbing his chin in deep thought. "This is a big decision," he said. "We must find out which scribe school would be best for you."

Hilal was apprehensive now that he had permission to go on his big adventure and the enormity of his decision began sinking in. He would be leaving all that he knew, leaving his family behind.

"I know of a great scribe called Hillel; he buys our skins and said I could go talk to him, that he would help me. I met him at our village market."

"Then it is settled," his father said determinedly. "I will give you my words to take to him and ask him to teach you his ways. Your uncle will be leaving in two days to go to the Holy City with skins. I will ask him to take you and deliver you to Hillel."

After a slight pause he added, "Now go back to your mother; tell her to prepare a feast for tomorrow night. I will bring our herd in tomorrow. Tell all of our people that this is a celebration... to wish you well on your journey. Be on your way now, son, before your mother gets more distraught."

Hilal was catching his father's excitement and rushed over to his father, wrapping his arms around him. He then turned the hug into a traditional Bedouin greeting, kissing him on each cheek before saying, "Thank you, Father."

He turned to start his journey back to the village, as he was disappearing from sight, his father returned to the campfire, tears streaming down his face. As he settled next to the campfire to pour another cup of coffee, Thanoon appeared from the darkness, startling him. "Brother, do you have any of that coffee left?" he asked.

Hilal's father jumped in surprise and tried to hide his tears, wiping them from his face. "Yes, of course. Then asking indignantly, what are you doing here?"

"Watching our boy. Your wife asked me to follow him and keep him safe."

Thanoon joined Hilal's father, accepting a cup of coffee. Thanoon lifted the cup to his mouth.

"Quickly... You must make haste and be on your way, Thanoon; watch over Hilal. I will return to our village in two days."

Thanoon was a little surprised with his curt dismissal, but realized this must be a difficult time for a father, letting a son follow his destiny, especially when away from the family.

Thanoon parted with, "Peace be with you." But Hilal's father was too preoccupied to answer as Thanoon was swallowed by the night.

THE CHOSEN ONE

JERUSALEM

Not wishing to waste any time, Thanoon went straight to the school where Hillel taught. "Greetings, Hillel!" he boomed as he recognized the scribe. "I have brought you the parchment skins you bought in our market in Wadi Zuballa."

They approached each other, arms spread wide in anticipation of a greeting among friends. "I also have a favor to ask you," Thanoon said. "I have a nephew who has seen you in our local market and wants to become a scribe – to enter your school to learn your ways."

"Is he the Bedouin boy I saw at the market in Wadi Zuballa?"

Thanoon shook his head yes.

"Is he Christian?"

"No, he is a Bedouin from the desert, the son of my sister."

Hillel dropped his head, quiet for a moment as if in deep thought. "Many years ago, it was foretold that a non-Jew would present himself to our school. It's possible that he might be the one."

Thanoon looked surprised. "The one? I do not understand."

"It is the story of the Jews and the Romans; it was foretold that during the coming of the Messiah, tensions would rise so that the Romans would ransack and pillage the Holy City. The vision explained that a rabbi – a man of the desert – would become the chosen one and that he would organize a campaign to save the history of the Jews from the invading Romans."

Hillel got up from his seated position, turning to Thanoon. "I will go get you your gold for the skins. Send your nephew to me tomorrow morning. We will have to see."

ONE CHANCE

Hilal did not sleep well. His uncle had told him he would get to talk to the Master Scribe Hillel in the morning. What if they did not accept him? They had to accept him, that was all there was to it, Hilal told his subconscious. He tossed and turned all night, seeming to only fall into a deep sleep minutes before his uncle woke him.

At last it was time. Thanoon led the very nervous Hilal to the entrance of the Temple Mount. They entered the huge plaza, in the center of which stood the Temple. The courtyard was surrounded by colonnades on all four sides. Hilal had never seen such majesty. He walked up the steps to the Temple and turned around to look at his uncle for reassurance.

Thanoon was still there, "It is alright, Hilal. You will do fine; go on in."

Hilal pushed open the big doors that dwarfed him, looking around for Hillel. The inside was even grander, and he was overwhelmed by the surroundings. He spotted Hillel waiving him over. "You are Hilal, the nephew of Thanoon?"

Hilal nodded, unable to voice his response.

"Do you have any idea of the dedication necessary to become a scribe?"

Hilal was so overawed, he just shook his head yes.

Hillel realized how overwhelmed the boy must be, and in a gentler tone, said, "Come sit down on my mat. You have much to learn."

After they were both seated, Hillel picked up a reed pen. He carefully drew a hieroglyphic in Ancient Aramaic on a piece of parchment. Next to it, with a quick sweep of his hand, he drew the same sign in Hebrew. He showed it to Hilal.

"Do you see the difference?"

Hilal studied the shapes and nodded his head. The old scribe paused, "As a scribe, you are given great power; the knowledge of hieroglyphics is a gargantuan responsibility.

"First, you must learn the script of the common man so you can perform everyday tasks. When you become proficient, if you are studious and learn well, you will study the sacred script. Those who learn the sacred script will learn the secrets of the gods and the mysteries of our people."

He paused again then turned around and brought out a small wooden palette. He held it out to the boy. "This is for you. If you learn to read and write, you will have many opportunities in the world. Study your signs well and you will go far."

He looked piercingly into the boy's eyes to stress the importance of his next question. "Hilal, do you want to join my school?"

The boy managed to squeak out, "Yes."

""If you pass a test, I will give you a chance. One month from today, if you can recite, read, and write the Ten Commandments, I will let you enter my school."

Hilal didn't have any difficulty finding his tongue now, with the awesome challenge facing him he stammered, "But...but..."

It was too late; Hillel had risen from the reed mat and walked off, calling over his shoulder, "One month, I will be waiting..."

DESTINY AND DECISION

THE TEMPLE MOUNT - JERUSALEM - 69 A.D.

"The Romans are entering the Temple compound; their patrols are getting closer and closer!"

Hilal sat at his station, having become an accomplished scribe and rabbi in his own right. He looked at the panicked junior scribe. The Temple Mount had been hallowed grounds for many centuries. Most outsiders, out of respect, would stay away, but the Romans had been purposefully disrespecting the Jewish law for some time, trespassing on sacred grounds, infuriating the Jewish community.

Hilal's daily routine was to work at his wooden desk translating and duplicating ancient texts until around the middle of the day. Then he was able to indulge his other true passion. After he had arrived in Jerusalem, while still a boy, he had asked the Master Scribe Hillel if he could help him find out where to go to learn some skills so that when he went back to Wadi Zuballa the bullies would not be able to humiliate him anymore.

Hillel had introduced Hilal to a school in Jerusalem that taught the Ancient Greek fighting skill of pankration – a combat sport introduced into the Greek Olympic Games in 648 B.C. and founded as a blend of boxing and wrestling with scarcely any rules. In Greek mythology, it was said that the heroes Hercules and Theseus invented pankration and that Theseus used his extraordinary skills to defeat the dreaded Minotaur in the Labyrinth while Hercules subdued the Nemean lion using pankration.

Hilal was now a true master of pankration in both the art of hand-to-hand combat and also with knives. His teacher had confided in the old Scribe Hillel that he thought the boy was probably even better than Hercules ever thought of being. Such was the dedication of Hilal to succeed.

And so, he was calm in the face of the flustered young scribe.

As Hilal tried to calm the young man, the large wooden doors to the Temple were suddenly kicked in, and ten Roman Centurions marched arrogantly inside. They pushed people aside until they managed to get close to Hilal. He knew this was a clear provocation, but he didn't react. The Romans' real purpose, he knew, was to incite an ill-advised response so they would have an excuse to retaliate.

The leader of the Roman troop shouted threateningly at the top of his voice, "Where is the Chief Rabbi?"

Hilal, although under orders not to antagonize the heathens, answered in a voice so low it was almost a whisper, "We are not deaf, soldier; we can hear quite well, thank you."

The leader must have also been under orders not to start a fight unless provoked. His face turned crimson and he chewed on his gums while thinking of a response. Eventually, in a most arrogant fashion, he replied, "I am not a soldier; I am a Roman Centurion. Where is the Chief Rabbi?"

Hilal responded gently in his low voice, "I don't know; I am but a junior scribe."

"Tell the Rabbi that General Titus wants to see him!" the soldier shouted. They turned to leave, kicking everything out of their path as they did.

LATER THAT DAY

The visit by the Roman soldiers put Hilal behind in his work, so he was still at his work desk in the early afternoon when he received another visitor. This man he did not recognize, nor did he hear him enter the sanctuary or approach.

Suddenly, the man was just there in front of Hilal, looking at him. But the stranger did know his name, and in the gentlest of voices, he asked, "Come sit with me, Hilal."

Scared to death, Hilal looked quizzically at the stranger. The man turned and walked a few paces to a reed mat on the floor, and Hilal followed.

"Once your teacher was known as Gavrel," the stranger closed his eyes, remembering as if the tale was etched in his subconscious. "He was a young student then, and he, too, received a visit from a stranger as he was at work in the Temple.

"You see, Hilal, the stranger told Gavrel that his destiny had two parts. The first was to take Moses' Torah out of Jerusalem to safety in Cypress. The second was that, upon his return from Cypress, he was to be patient and wait.

"One day, a young Bedouin from the desert would present himself at Gavrel's school. This Bedouin was to secret away all the sacred writings of Jewish history before the Romans ransacked and burned Jerusalem to the ground."

The stranger looked piercingly at him, "Your time has come, Hilal."

Hilal was overwhelmed to think that plans had been in place since before he was born, but he had a destiny of his own.

"Why didn't Gavrel also hide the scared writings?" he asked.

"Moses' Torah was a finished work. It had the Ten Commandments written by God himself and given to Moses on Mount Sinai. This was the foundation of the Jewish faith; it had to be preserved for the future.

The kind-faced stranger looked intently at Hilal. "But God knew he had sent his son to do his work, and that all of the writings of the works of Jesus were not yet written. He would need another young man when that time came, so he had Gavrel prepare you for your destiny."

It was all so much to take in. Hilal sat stunned, staring at the stranger. The young rabbi shuddered. He felt a strange sensation running down his spine. This genteel messenger was dressed in a robe with a hood pushed back from his face, revealing long white hair brushed back behind his neck and green compassionate eyes in a face that had many wrinkles, as if the stranger had spent a lifetime smiling.

The man paused while Hilal thought this through. "Soon the Romans will destroy Jerusalem. We must be ready. Now you must make plans to get our precious scrolls – our history – to safety. It is time."

Hilal was having none of this. This diversion was not part of his plan to return to Wadi Zuballa almost immediately. He already had a destiny – to go home to Wadi Zuballa, become an Elder on the Council of Elders and then rise to the leadership of the council. This is what had driven him these many years, he thought to himself.

"I have just received word that my father is very ill," he explained. "I must go to him. It is my duty."

He was defiant. A plan held dear and nurtured for 25 years or more was not easily discarded.

The stranger looked at him compassionately, nodding his head in understanding, the deep wrinkles in his face smiling back at the young scribe in a most sincere expression.

It seemed he totally comprehended the internal conflict the young man was experiencing. "Hilal, it is not your father's time. God needs you," the stranger reiterated in the softest of tones.

"My destiny is to lead my tribe; I promised my father."

Although Hilal was unconvinced, the stranger insisted, gently, as if he had not heard a word of what the young man said, "The Romans are coming; they will burn the Temple. If they find the words of God, our sacred history, they will burn that, too."

Hilal was shocked; he had been studying, translating and duplicating the original commandments from God and the many interpretations of them for many years. More recently, a lot of his work had been recording the words of the Messiah. The importance of protecting hundreds of years of history and sacred writings was such an immense responsibility that he simply couldn't ignore it.

As the enormity of the situation settled on his shoulders, he turned to the stranger with a puzzled look on his face. "Why did he change his name from Gavrel to Hillel?"

The stranger smiled. "There are two answers to that. The first is that the

Sadducees' high priest was fit to be tied when he learned that Lazarus had escaped. In fact, he was so furious that he demanded the head of the leader of the conspirators in Seulecia be brought to him on a platter. The only crime this obedient ruffian had committed was to give Lazarus a leaky boat, obeying his orders."

The stranger continued, "He was not satisfied with that. He also wanted to know who the person was that rescued Lazarus and Barnabus in the harbor. The first mate of the brig innocently told them Gavrel had chartered the boat. The high priests had their people search high and low for Gavrel, but couldn't find him. He had, in the meantime, changed his name to Hillel.

"But the high priest was not the forgiving sort. He reported Gavrel to the Romans, and they put a price on his head. He is still on their wanted list. That is why he had to change his name so that he could wait for you here in Jerusalem to train you."

"And the second?"

"The second answer is that Gavrel asked me for the name of the Bedouin he awaited. I answered 'Hilal,' and he replied 'I will never remember that name.' So, since he had to change his name anyway, we decided on Hillel, to help him remember your name."

Hilal chuckled at the irony of the story. He was resigned to this new fate. "What must I do?" he asked.

The stranger was again smiling paternally at Hilal. "You know the way," the stranger responded in the form of a riddle, then pointed to the Moses seat.

"Go there; your destiny awaits you."

Hilal walked grudgingly the few paces to the seat and sat down, looking for answers. He turned around to talk to the stranger, but he was alone.

THANOON GOES TO QUMRAN

JERUSALEM HOME OF HILAL

"My Uncle, we are running out of time. I have been reading some of the words of Jesus. Even he says the Romans are going to ransack Jerusalem," Hilal said. He and Thanoon sat on a reed mat sharing tea, planning their strategy to remove the artifacts from besieged Jerusalem.

"In one of the scriptures I was translating, he said to one of his disciples, 'Truly I tell you, not one stone here will be left on another; every one will be thrown down.'"

Thanoon nodded. "On my way into town, I hardly recognized the old Jerusalem. Most of the trees have been cut down by the Romans, houses torched. Rumor has it that Titus is going to have a wall constructed around the entire city of Jerusalem so that no one can go in and no one can go out.

"They say this wall will be as high as the other defensive walls of the city. If that happens, all hope for escape for the Jews will be cut off," Thanoon said.

Hilal was listening intently to the latest gossip his uncle had picked up.

"Uncle, these things the Romans are doing have all been foretold by Jesus. One of the scrolls I was working on quoted Jesus as saying. *'For the days shall come upon you when your enemies will throw up a bank before you, and surround you, and hem you in on every side.'*

"I think it is time to move, Uncle. Jesus has warned us; you have heard the rumors. You must make a trip to Qumran. We will have to make two trips, the first with the supplies and the scrolls we brought here from the surrounding synagogues."

Thanoon interrupted his nephew; he didn't understand the reason for two trips. "Why two trips, Nephew? Couldn't we wait and make one trip?"

Hilal shook his head. "The rest of the scrolls are hidden in the Temple. We have to be so careful; the Romans are watching everything. If they discover me bringing the Temple scrolls here, we could lose everything. Better move these to safety first."

Hilal reached into his bag and pulled out an old scroll to give to Thanoon. His uncle unfolded it, spreading it out in front of them. When he saw it was a map, he was indignant.

"My Nephew, I don't need a map! I am a Bedouin trader; I have been traveling the desert for many years. The stars are my guide. Why, I have never been lost on any of my trips! Why I have travelled..."

Hilal had to cut his uncle off or his tirade would last all day. Thanoon had the one common flaw that most lone travelers of the desert carried – they were tired of talking to camels. So when they reached civilization, they would monopolize conversations, talk incessantly, go on forever.

"Uncle," he started loudly, trying to break in, "this is very important. If you cannot locate the cave from the stars, please take this map and use the sun to locate the cave on the summer solstice."

Thanoon grudgingly took the map and scowled at his nephew for cutting him off. Why, I was just getting started, he thought. If only my nephew knew of the exciting places I have travelled to!

Hilal was in a hurry; he had no time to spend on pleasantries. "Uncle, we must pack all your camels tonight so you are ready to leave first thing in the morning. I must get back to the Temple Mount in the morning to continue to remove more scrolls."

Reluctantly, Thanoon got to work preparing his cargo for transport. Before first light, he was ready, camels loaded, starting the trek toward the East Gate for the trip across the Negev desert.

THE TRAIL TO QUMRAN

Safely outside the East Gate, Thanoon and his caravan of camels began the long trek to Qumran. The ancient trail sloped gradually down between barren hills interspersed with occasional camps. Some of these camps were desert-dwelling Bedouins and some were refugees from Jerusalem who had heeded the warnings of Jesus and left while they still could.

The trail Thanoon took slowly descended more than 3,600 feet, finally to a depth of more than 1,000 feet below sea-level. The heat concentrated in this below-sea-level Mecca was oppressive, but the view on all sides was mesmerizing, from the Jordan Valley on one side to Jericho on the other, both undulating in a hazy mirage. And in that haze, beyond the Dead Sea, stood the majesty of the mountains of Moab.

Thanoon loved the beauty and majesty of the desert, finding the serenity of the place spellbinding – different terrains, sands and mountains and fertile oasis and sense of true timelessness. By mid-morning the next day, his caravan entered the wadi meant to lead to Hilal's cave.

HILAL'S CAVE

After following the wadi for the afternoon, the base of the river bed began to climb, and he entered the mountains of Qumran. He started looking for the tell-tale signs of Hilal's magical cave. He searched and searched, but to no avail.

Finally, he tethered his camels and began to search on foot. He followed the bank of each side, examining every possibility, even scratching himself up on numerous thorn bushes. He was beginning to think that perhaps his nephew was playing with him. He half expected to see the boy jump out and tease him about his navigating skills.

"If this is a joke, I will get even with my nephew. I have been traveling the desert for many decades and have never gotten lost, not even when I was traveling in a sandstorm," he bellowed angrily to the empty desert.

The first night, he made camp with a small open fire. He thought the night would never pass. He couldn't sleep, afraid of losing his precious cargo, and the sounds of mountain goats or some other animal jarring loose stones kept disturbing him.

On the beginning of the second day, he decided he must get his supplies and scrolls out of the desert sun. As he sought shelter, he climbed under a rock, and to his surprise, found a secret entrance to another cavern. He started to dig and dig to widen it out.

What he found was a natural underground passageway. As he dug down to clear the sand, he scraped the side of what appeared to be a limestone opening he could crawl through. Inside was a cave big enough to store all of his provisions and scrolls out of the sun.

Thanoon unloaded all of his supplies and scrolls, walking from his camels to the cavern carrying it all. After he was satisfied, he hobbled his camels and crawled back into the cavern to sleep. The next morning, he crawled out of his secret cavern to resume his search for Hilal's cave. He covered up the entrance to his hideaway and grudgingly pulled out Hilal's map from his breast pocket.

The directions were very specific. He studied the map some more, then as was his habit, he spoke to El Deloua, his favorite camel. "I have had enough of this foolishness, Del. If this is some game my nephew is playing …"

He grumbled to himself as he studied the map but made little sense of it. "I will wait for the mid-day sun to show me the way."

Thanoon was clearly getting very angry. Even in his anger, the very idea that he could be mistaken never crossed his mind. He was almost regal, he was so sure of himself. "If I can't find it, then it can't be there," he decided, talking to himself.

At mid-day, Thanoon continued his search, consulting the map again. "I will follow the directions to the letter. My nephew is an accomplished rabbi. If I am wrong, my sister and brother-in-law will tease me unmercifully for years to come. I'd better follow the directions exactly."

He looked at the map, this time following the instructions. He began to climb up a limestone outcropping featured prominently on the map. It indicated that he should be in position to observe the sun shine through a small weathered opening in a limestone cliff. He waited and waited, all the time scanning the cliffs in front of him for any opening. He couldn't see it.

The sun rose, he waited impatiently. Thanoon was talking to no one, but his mutterings gave him comfort, "If I am the laughingstock of the next family gathering... I will get even. What a cruel joke."

He was still rambling to himself when a laser like ray of sunlight shone through the rock opening he was looking at and thrust its light on a shiny stone behind a thorn bush on the ground where he had been standing earlier.

Thanoon was so surprised that he lost his footing and went sliding down the rock face. The further down the rock he slid, the more his robe was pushed up so that his buttocks were exposed to the gritty rock surface. As he went down, his cheeks were rubbed raw by the gravel over which he rode. Moments later, he came to a stop at the bottom of the gorge, rubbing his very sore and tender bottom.

As he stood, lamenting the bruised condition of his rear end, he looked in amazement at the entrance to a secret cave hidden behind the thorn bush. Thanoon's shock was total; there it was. He had been looking at it all the time, an opening to a cave, perfectly cloaked, hidden in plain sight, only visible if you happened to be looking at the right place from the correct angle.

HILAL'S CAVE

Thanoon walked toward the cave slowly, almost reverently, and peered at the entrance. He could see that the cave was deep and went further than the light would let him examine.

"I will need a lamp," he said aloud, heading back to his supplies to get an oil lantern. As he approached the entrance to the cave from outside again, it narrowed immediately so only one man or camel could pass at a time. When he entered, strange shadows appeared, projected by his lamp, making things eerie.

The entrance curved sharply, before opening into a larger passageway. Thanoon was a man of the open desert, and confined, dark places where his vision was impaired scared him. Before he went any further, he knelt to the ground to see if he could recognize any tracks or droppings. He crawled around, examining the ground.

"Hmmmm. A gazelle and a large cat – probably a Caracal – maybe some jackals. I had better be armed before I go further," he said.

Thanoon went back to his camel to get his sword and a lance to probe in front of him in case a large cat surprised him.

Back in the cave, he first inspected the entrance from the inside, and it looked like someone had spent a lot of time modifying the cave to protect the inhabitants from intruders. A large recess had been cut into the upper side that still housed enough big, heavy rocks to close off the opening. The rocks were still there, and it looked like one log-shaped rock at the bottom of the pile was securing all of them. If that was pulled, the pile of rocks would be released, closing the entrance off from the world outside.

Overhead, a thin furrow had been cut or chiseled, as if designed so someone could wedge in animal skins to close off the inhabitants from the night. Thanoon started to explore, and found an oasis of treasures. On the walls were not only engravings of hippo, giraffe, elephants, and lions, but also some long-horned, cow-like animal he had never seen before. He thought to himself, what are etchings of reptilian crocodiles – which he had only seen in drawings on his travels – doing in the middle of the desert?

The ceilings of the cave were covered in dark charcoal residual, indicating years of habitation. A natural spring fed a small rock pool with fresh water. He continued to explore, re-creating the layout of the ancient residents. A stable was located to the rear to store fodder and dried animal dung for the fire. From the fresh water that dripped into a pool at the front of the cave, a small trench had been dug to provide water to the living area.

Closer to the middle of the cave was a tunnel large enough for a camel to pass through that led up an incline to a dry storage area. The living quarters were closer to the front, still far enough back from the entrance so a fire could not be seen from the outside. The walls were covered with paintings of animals and people. A river was etched on the wall, as well as thick vegetation.

He started to clean out centuries of residue from the pool to discover an ancient sluice gate made out of rock. When elevated, it allowed water to flow down a small canal to the trench in the stable area. After seeing the size of the internal cave, Thanoon decided to go back outside to get his camels and hide them from any people that might pass by.

As he led his camels into the hidden lair, he marveled at the majesty of it all. He was absolutely taken aback. He realized that all the drawings on the walls meant this cave was inhabited thousands of years ago when the desert must have been home to much more water and different plants and animals. A paradise none of his people had ever seen.

Thanoon was very proud of himself; he had found the cave. He wasn't sure whether he would tell Hilal the undignified manner in which he made the discovery, but nevertheless, he had found it. He decided to make it as comfortable as possible. By the end of the day, he had transferred all the supplies from his cave into this one, and he only used El Deloua, leaving the other camels in the stable area of Hilal's cave.

He now had all the comforts of home here, forage for the camels and weeks of supplies. He decided he would rest and work on getting the scrolls and Hilal's other supplies another day; he was tired.

Thanoon spread out a carpet close to the fire, laid back and closed his eyes. El Deloua was with him, lying next to the fire. He leaned against her. The sudden silence was miraculous, each tiny sound in the stillness amplified by the rock walls. He opened his eyes to see the flickering fire illuminating rock art etched thousands of years ago. As the fire mellowed, darkness enveloped the cavern, so total. Through that blackness, minuscule flame outs from the dung fire cast eerie shadows, highlighting different drawings.

Thanoon was slightly overawed by his new surroundings, and he spoke out loud to El Deloua, "I smell the sweet pungent aroma of burned droppings. I don't know whether that is you or the fire." He laughed to himself.

El Deloua seemed to know that he was talking to her, and she grunted. They both settled down to sleep, and as night progressed, their silence was only interrupted by an occasional grunt from El Deloua. Later, he awoke in the darkness, disturbed by the sounds he heard of the faint trickle of spring water dripping into the fresh water rock pool. The splash was suddenly loud, a constant irritant, until it became just another noise of the night.

After that, Thanoon slept peacefully for the rest of the night, until his head bumped hard suddenly on the carpet-covered rock floor. El Deloua had decided to get up and stretch her legs to get some water from the stable area at the back of the cave. He rose then, realizing it must be morning, and he had overslept. He rubbed the swelling on the back of his head as he turned to look around him.

A faint light was filtering in from the entrance, so he knew it was time to get moving. He added some kindling to the fire to brew some tea then walked out of the cave, stretching and yawning.

As reality set in, he started to pay more attention. He looked around to see if anyone was observing him. Seeing no one outside the cave, he approached some bushes and was about to relieve himself, when he heard from the rocky slope above him, "Hello, Uncle."

Thanoon jumped as much as he could in his compromised position, He was startled and whirled around while busy trying to regain his dignity. He was a little miffed to say the least. "Hilal, I wish you wouldn't do that! If you weren't so big I would put you over my knee."

It didn't help Thanoon's mood that Hilal was laughing so hard that he, too, nearly lost his footing on the rock ledge where he perched.

Hilal was still enjoying every moment of his surprise when he added merrily, "Uncle, I arrived so late last night I didn't want to disturb you. I heard you and your bedfellow snoring so loudly, I thought it prudent to wait till morning to greet you."

Thanoon still had not recovered enough to be his normal jovial self, but he was trying. "That was, El Deloua. She snores very loudly, but she is a good companion and a very soft pillow."

Hilal expressed genuine surprise; he didn't know whether his uncle could have been hiding a secret love all this time and managed to get her here with him. "I'll look forward to meeting her – El Deloua, you say? Is she spoiled rotten?"

"Come into my cave and share some tea with me; I have just stoked the fire, the water is probably already boiling." Thanoon turned and started toward the cave entrance, leading Hilal.

"You know, Uncle, this must have been an incredible place when the original inhabitants lived here. Can you imagine walking out of this entrance to go hunt all these animals on the wall?"

Thanoon nodded his head in agreement. "I would like to know what happened to that wonderful landscape to turn it into a dry desert."

"I don't think we will ever know," Hilal answered.

They both sat down on carpets around the fire to enjoy their tea. Thanoon was easily distracted and didn't want to spend any more time talking about the cave; he wanted to talk about something more important to him.

"Have I ever told you about El Deloua?"

Hilal knew his uncle well and was not going to let him go off on a tangent. If he did, he would talk for hours about El Deloua.

"No, I don't, but first tell me about your work in the caves."

Thanoon switched topics dutifully. "I followed your directions exactly of course and found the cave very easily."

Hilal was not convinced that it was that easy. "So you found the cave without difficulty or did you have to use my map?"

Thanoon was subconsciously rubbing his bottom, not willing to lie to his nephew. "Of course I used your map; you made me promise. Yes, I did. Your directions were perfect."

Hilal was all business; he was looking around at everything Thanoon had brought into the cave. "I don't see my scrolls here."

Thanoon looked over at the provisions. "I have not brought them in here yet. When I first arrived here, I wanted to get your scrolls out of the sun. I found a small cavern close by where I could store things while I followed your directions to find this cave."

"Good," answered Hilal. "So everything is safe?"

"Everything is safely stored, hidden from prying eyes."

"Good. Now, tell me about your companion."

Now, Thanoon was beaming; he finally got to talk about what he wanted to talk about. "I have been roaming the desert alone for so long now, as you know. I was getting very lonely. At night, I would constantly dream of the perfect companion. I made a mental list of the features I found most attractive – sultry eyes, long eye lashes, strong, long legs, not overweight. She would have to keep up with me, of course."

He was off in his dream world, and Hilal just smiled and listened, but he was thinking that from the volume of the snoring he heard last night, it would be interesting to meet this 'delicate' female.

His uncle continued, "She would also have to learn to listen to my wise counsel and definitely not talk too much. Then on one trip, the most amazing thing happened, after traveling through the night, I was approaching the outskirts of Aqaba. For some reason, El Deloua was standing along the side road watching me. When I spotted her, it was love at first sight.

"That is how El Deloua, 'the spoiled one,' came into my life," Thanoon beamed. "If it wasn't love at first sight, I would never have paid such a large dowry – a relative fortune. Now she is my constant companion."

He heard a noise from the interior of the cave and looked around. Hilal followed his uncle's gaze, but all he saw was a camel. Puzzled, he looked again at his uncle. "All I see is a camel; surely she is not the love of your life?"

Thanoon looked momentarily taken back, as if he could not imagine anyone not falling in love with his camel. He recovered quickly and said proudly, "Ah, there she is, my El Deloua."

His camel walked over to nuzzle him. Hilal was still smiling at his uncle.

"That's quite a story, Uncle," he said politely, thinking his uncle never ceased to amaze him.

But Thanoon was not finished, he continued, rubbing her nose and ears, "We have travelled many miles together. At night, we share a campfire, and I lay up against her ample chest, watching the stars. I talk of my concerns, and she listens, chewing her cud. It is a great arrangement."

Now Thanoon was satisfied that he had told Hilal his story, and he returned to business. "Let me show you around," he offered.

They finished their tea, got up and Hilal followed Thanoon further into the cave. As they entered the storage area, Thanoon started his guided tour. "As you can imagine when I arrived here, I had to find a place out of the sun to store all your scrolls. I put everything in a cavern that I found that is not on your map. We can go there anytime and bring your supplies when you are ready. But first, My Nephew, one question..."

Thanoon stopped his tour and looked very seriously at Hilal, "Your family and I do not understand this quest you are on. The Council of Elders of your tribe is waiting for you to return to Wadi Zuballa to serve as our leader. Your father is the Elder of our tribe; it is your duty to come home to serve.

He stopped and looked solemnly at his nephew. "A Bedouin is always a Bedouin."

"You are right, Uncle. We must go to our village, and I must pay my respects to my family; it has been far too long. But first we must secure the cave."

Thanoon had another thought, "I also think it is time for you to tell me what we are doing in Qumran."

"I will answer all your questions in Wadi Zuballa at my father's house. In the meantime, we must hide all trace of our presence here."

DEFENDING DESTINY

HILAL'S HOME IN THE VILLAGE OF WADI ZUBALLA

Hilal and Thanoon had been traveling for two days when they sighted Wadi Zuballa.

It wasn't long after the pair spotted the village that the local dogs started barking. Village children, once alerted, ran toward the caravan. Adult members of the community flocked to them, as well, to learn the latest news or see what goods were for sale, but the village children had ulterior motives. Some of the regular traders who came to Wadi Zuballa were known and popular for different reasons, at least among the children. The trader who was most popular was Thanoon. Once El Deloua was spotted, the word spread, and it became a hectic race to see who could spot Thanoon first.

A throng of village children came running toward the approaching camels, and Hilal saw Thanoon dismount and walk to the back of the caravan. He wondered if something needed his uncle's attention. As the children approached, they shouted out almost in unison, "It's Thanoon's El Deloua! Where is Thanoon?"

More children joined the happy throng of greeters at the front of the caravan. They all started looking for Thanoon. They demanded of Hilal, "Where is Thanoon?"

No one recognized Hilal; it had been so long since he had been back to his birth village. He couldn't understand why children were clamoring for his uncle. They gave up asking Hilal, who had not answered, and started walking back along the caravan searching for Thanoon.

As the children were about to express their disappointment, he jumped out from behind the last camel. As usual he was ready for them. They ran up to him, shouting, "Thanoon! Thanoon! What did you bring us?"

Hilal had turned around to see what the excitement was about and was mystified. "Why are you so excited to see Thanoon?" he asked.

The children responded in the happiest of tones, "He always brings us the best treats! Dates soaked in sugar, yum!"

All the children ran toward the end of the caravan now, where a beaming Thanoon carried a sack of special treats. They screeched in joy as

47

they ran to him.

Hilal couldn't help but smile at Thanoon. "Everybody's uncle!" he joined in the shouting.

Later that day, Hilal and Thanoon were the guests of honor at his parents' home where Hilal's mother stoked the fire in the middle of the living area. Hilal, his father and Thanoon sat around the fire finishing their evening meal.

Steaming hot tea was served, and Hilal's father started off with a question, "Son, it has been a long time since you visited us. Fortunately, your uncle has kept us updated. Have you found a good Bedouin girl with which to bless us with grandchildren?"

"Only my Uncle has found the perfect companion," Hilal said, smiling.

His parents looked at him quizzically, and Thanoon looked as if to say, "Do not speak further."

Hilal couldn't resist as he half laughing said, "You know, El Deloua!"

Thanoon jumped up and launched himself onto Hilal, while his mother and father laughed unrestrainedly. He was mastering the friendly tussle. "I told you I would get you if you brought that up!"

Hilal was laughing so hard he couldn't defend himself. "Mercy, Uncle! Mercy!"

Thanoon and Hilal went back to their positions on the carpet still laughing. The family returned to savoring their sweet tea.

Then Hilal's father asked, "So, what of your destiny, son?"

He looked deeply into Hilal's eyes, almost piercing into his soul, so intent was his question.

"I understand your question, Father, but my journey has been remarkable, and it is not over."

"Son, for many years, Bedouin tribes have been ruled by a Council of Elders. As a Bedouin, it is your duty to take over my position to lead our people forward."

Hilal did not know how to answer his father; it would be very difficult for him to understand. "My journey has only just begun, Father."

Hilal's father did not understand; confused, he asked, "What can be more important than the future of our people?"

Hilal was torn by his loyalty to his family and to the old scribe, Hillel, the stranger and to his spiritual beliefs. "It is the history of a nation that I am destined to save," he said.

Thanoon was no help, he added to the confusion by saying, "I do not understand either, and I have been traveling with him."

Hilal's parents looked at each other, trying to see if either of them understood their son's position. Hilal decided there was only one way to go – tell them the whole story.

"Mother, Father, Uncle," he began, "let me try to explain. Bedouin tribes are ruled by a Council of Elders. Each tribal Council is ruled by the Supreme

Bedouin Council of Elders. That is how our society works."

They all nodded agreement, and Hilal felt relief. So far, so good.

"The Supreme Council of Elders is not worshipped as a god," he continued, "They are just men, not gods, but there is an Almighty One, a God of all people."

Hilal's mother interrupted, obviously interested now. "Who is he?"

"He is not of this world. This Almighty God tells us that no MAN should be worshipped as a god. There is no god, but one God alone."

Now it was his father's turn to interrupt. "How does this affect us?" he asked.

"The Romans believe their supreme leader, Caesar, is a god and all should worship him as the one god, but believers know that God's word expressly prohibits the worship of false idols. In order for the Romans to have all people worship Caesar as a god, they must destroy every last written word about the Almighty One and his teachings. The primary objective of the Romans marching on Jerusalem is to destroy the Torah. It is a sacred book – the Hebrew Bible – containing all the laws of the Jews…"

Now Thanoon asked, "Is the Torah in Jerusalem?"

No, my teacher together with some friends took the Torah out of Judea many years ago.

Hilal's mother thought that was good news, she innocently asked, "So you can come home to your family now?"

"Sadly no, Mother. The Torah is only part of the story. Over many years, the word of God has been translated by scribes into everyday rules for the common man. These sacred scrolls also must be saved from the Romans. Ever since God's only son, Jesus, was crucified by Pontius Pilate, tensions have been running very high."

"If the Torah is safe, why do you need to risk your life for these scrolls?" asked his father.

"Many of these writings now contain the words of Jesus Christ and his followers. From these scriptures, two distinct factions have developed. Both believe that the Almighty God exists, but the disagreement is now 'Who is God's chosen people?'

"The Jews believe that Jesus was the son of God on earth. The followers of Ishmael, the son of Abraham, believe that Jesus was just a man, teaching the word of God rather than the son of God on earth."

Thanoon was getting it. He asked, "So the common enemy for all of us is the Romans?"

Hilal was finally smiling, believing that he was getting his point across. "Yes, the Romans want to enslave us all, make us pay homage to Caesar."

"Are the Jews so sure of themselves that they would take on the military muscle of Rome?" his father asked.

"They have no choice," Hilal said sadly. "You must all stay here close to home. Much blood will be spilled."

His mother was indignant, "Who are these Romans?"

Hilal smiled at her, shaking his head. "That is the problem. The general in Judea is the son of the current Caesar, Titus Flavius Caesar Vespasianus Augustus. His son wants to prove himself worthy of taking over from his father, so he is taking extraordinarily brutal measures to become worthy of succession.

"Mother, I would like to stay. But my destiny is not here. God has chosen me to be the protector of the scriptures. I must return to Jerusalem to retrieve what I can before the Roman army destroys everything."

His mother and father exchanged concerned looks and then looked over to Thanoon, who, realizing what that look meant, nodded at them, saying, "I will be going with Hilal. Don't worry, I have taught our boy the ancient skill of the knives and he has become a master of pankration. I will look after him."

Hilal's father said, "If he is going to help defeat the Romans, he will have to be as good as Hercules! Is he?"

Thanoon, ever the loyal uncle replied, "Better."

BACK TO JERUSALEM

A sad day dawned in Wadi Zuballa as not only Hilal's family said goodbye to him and his uncle, but the village children bid farewell to their favorite person, Thanoon.

The pair mounted camels and was prepared to leave when some of the children ran up to them, shouting, "Thanoon! Thanoon! Are you leaving so soon?"

Thanoon did not favor prolonged goodbyes. He told them sternly, "Go back to your homes! Yes, I have important business to attend to. Go home!"

"When are you coming back?" they asked.

Thanoon said in a conspiratorial whisper, "I don't know, children. You know how it is with important business; sometimes you don't know how long it is going to take."

"Will you bring more treats when you come?"

Thanoon tried to glare at them menacingly, but was not very successful. "Of course. Now go home! Go on all of you! I'll be back soon enough."

The children laughed and scampered off happily.

The barren expanse of desert in front of them as they rode out of town was a stark contrast to the warm family environment they had just left. Both were immersed in their own thoughts as they plodded on. It was Hilal who first broke the silence, asking a question that had been nagging him – always at the back of his mind.

"By the way, Thanoon, you never told me where you hid the scrolls in Qumran. Is it close to the main cave?"

Thanoon was not even thinking about Hilal and his cave. He was truly worried about the magnitude of the task in front of them; it seemed as if it was just the two of them up against the entire Roman Army.

After tugging his mind back to Hilal's question, he answered, "Yes, very close, Nephew, a thirty-minute walk at the most."

After he had responded, he tried to think about how he could direct Hilal to the cave where the scrolls were hidden, and realized that he could not. He would have to be there to show his nephew.

Hilal was thinking the same thing to himself, concerned whether he would be able to find the right place alone. "Could you mark it on the map I gave you?"

Thanoon had hoped Hilal wouldn't ask him that, as he was not a man of letters like his nephew and had a hard time using Hilal's map in the first place. He thought to himself, I am a man of the stars, my father taught me how to navigate around our desert; we never have had a use for maps.

"I think I could, but better I just show you," he said instead.

Hilal knew better than to argue with his uncle, thinking that Thanoon and maps did not get on well together. Still, he did start to get that uncomfortable feeling in the pit of his stomach. He would wish later on that he had paid more attention to that gut feeling then.

They both returned to their own thoughts until they got close to the outskirts of Jerusalem. The remaining journey was a quiet one with Hilal worried about all he had to accomplish and Thanoon very uneasy going back into the middle of a war-torn town.

On the second day of their journey, El Deloua was the first to notice, and raised her head, nostrils flapping, grunting, to alert them that something was upsetting her. The desert camel had very sharp vision and hearing, as well as a strong sense of smell. Thanoon had known El Deloua to sense water from nearly two miles away, so he had an acute respect for her abilities.

He noticed her change of mood and asked her, "What is it Del?"

Thanoon raised his eyes to the horizon around Jerusalem, and saw there was more smoke than usual. Hilal saw Thanoon's sudden attention to the horizon, and he too started to look inquisitively. "What do you see, Uncle?"

It took Thanoon some minutes to finish his look around. When he did, he answered, "It's what I don't see that worries me."

He pointed up into the sky, and Hilal followed his gaze. It seemed like out of nowhere, thousands of vultures had suddenly appeared and circled overhead. The pair continued their journey forward and it wasn't long before they, too, could smell what had disturbed El Deloua – the stench of rotting flesh. The closer they got to Jerusalem, the more repugnant it became.

As they approached the outskirts, they began to see more devastation and destruction. All the trees around the city – the beautiful, green, wooded areas – were gone. Only stumps and desert remained. The old suburbs of Jerusalem full of glorious parks and green areas were now smoldering eyesores, and thousands of bodies lay all around rotting in the sun.

The smell of rotten flesh was unbearable, a sweet, sickly, putrid aroma attracting flies and vultures by the thousands. Packs of dogs and jackals feasted on the decaying human flesh. Many of the stomachs were bloated by the heat until the gases were released by the puncturing fangs of the ravaging dogs.

Thanoon and Hilal both adjusted their head clothes to put a cover over their nose and mouth. Hundreds of people hung along the side of the road, crucified crudely on the only trees left standing.

"I hear that General Titus has ordered all prisoners to be crucified,"

Hilal said. "Some say hundreds of souls have been crucified each day in the Mount of Olives. That is also why there are no trees standing; those that haven't been chopped down to make ramparts for the siege, were used to crucify Jews."

As they got closer to town, they saw more bodies, so many that the jackals and wild dogs could not keep up. Many bodies had been simply gutted, their stomachs sliced open.

"Why would they gut these defenseless souls?" Thanoon asked. "What type of animal would do that?"

Hilal answered, his face showing the total revulsion he felt, "Many of the Jews had swallowed their money as they tried to escape. When the Roman soldiers discovered this, many of them simply cut open every prisoner's stomach hoping to find a reward."

Thanoon looked appalled. "What has happened here? This must be hell! How could the largest empire in the world stoop to these lows? Never in my wildest imagination did I even consider such cruelty."

He put a hand across the space to touch Hilal. "My Nephew, if I ever had any doubt about helping you in your quest, be sure, I do not now. I will do whatever I can to wipe these barbarians from the face of the earth."

They rode on. Thanoon said thoughtfully, "You told me that you knew this was going to happen. How did you know?"

"You forget I am a scribe; my duties are not only to protect the scriptures, but to copy many of these writings for others to read."

Hilal pointed to the Mount of Olives above Jerusalem. "One of the scrolls I was copying told of a meeting between Jesus and his disciples only a few days before he was crucified. They were on the Mount of Olives, overlooking the Temple, and Jesus said to them,

"You see all these, do you not? Truly, I say to you, there will not be left here one stone upon another, that will not be thrown down."

"He was talking about Jerusalem," Hilal said. "He warned us about all this. What you see here are the many who did not believe his words."

Soldiers stood formally at all crucial intersections in shining bronze helmets with Mohawk like red hair, shields clasped to their chests and swords banging on their shields. Smoldering embers of destroyed residences lined the suburbs, the stench of charred lumber and rotten corpses overpowering. Bodies lay where they were slaughtered. Any survivors were skinny, hair matted, eyes wide and frightened in dirty rags instead of clothes.

In front of the walls of Jerusalem, monolithic wooden structures on wheels still stood ready. The outskirts of the city were being put to the torch, every structure in sight set on fire. Locals who tried to defend their property were put to the sword. Not a stone was left unturned as the Romans systematically destroyed everything in their path, readying for the final push to breach the walls and invade the inner sanctum of Jerusalem to destroy the second Temple.

THE SIEGE BEGINS

As if awaiting Hilal and Thanoon, the attack on Temple Mount began. The little, provoked skirmishes became full-fledged, brutal assaults. In a savage confrontation, the Romans broke through the city's walls again, as Christians rushed to try to repair the gaps. Hurrying to fortify all they could around the temple, they tried to strengthen defenses before it was all set afire and destroyed. People retreated from the dreaded Romans, running back toward the Temple and looking over their shoulders at the advancing barbarians.

Once they got there, they realized there was nowhere else to go; there was no more room for the late arrivals. As the final defenses were breached, flames began to feast on the wooden structures.

Suddenly the defenders realized this was the end. Out of desperation, came a surge of renewed effort, and they threw themselves against the invaders. Now they were fighting two enemies – the Romans and the fire. As the flames rose, Christians screamed in agony. They had fire to their back, swords to their front, and were slaughtered by the thousands.

The wailing of the dying and the striking of sword against bone and stone was deafening. The fire was so hot and so intense that the victims were quickly consumed, the smell of burning flesh nauseating.

Thanoon and Hilal watched from a distance, feeling tremendous guilt because there was nothing they could do. In the fury of battle, 6,000 were left dead or dying from their efforts to defend Temple Mount. But even this was not enough; the Romans wanted to destroy, to obliterate everything. In only minutes, the sanctuary was reached and desecrated. Roman soldiers plundered the treasury, carrying off anything of value including Hilal's gold-plated duplicates. Anything not of value was put to the torch or pummeled into nothingness. Jerusalem was ransacked and burned. The Temple was gone.

Thanoon and Hilal watched the devastation, unbelieving. They saw a contingent of Titus' personal guards haul off the most valuable treasures. Even from this distance, they could see the menorah – the golden candlestick – and the table of the shewbread, as well as a smaller sack full of incense cups. The golden candlestick was so heavy and magnificent that six guards struggled to carry it. The troops took off in the direction of Titus' camp on the Mount of Olives.

The Roman soldiers carried their treasures through the camp on the Mount of Olives, passing smoldering campfires and simple tents, until they arrived at the luxurious enclosure of General Titus. The flap was thrown back, and the soldiers struggled to bring in the golden candlestick, the table of the shewbread and the smaller sack full of incense cups.

General Titus walked into this room to survey his booty. He was surrounded by the Roman soldiers who carried in the loot and his Adjutant Flavius, a battle-hardened warrior with a deep scar running from the right side of his forehead to his chin.

General Titus ordered Flavius, "Fetch my goldsmith; I want to know how much gold I have here!"

"Yes, Sire."

General Titus had a reputation as a very cruel master and had been known to strike down a subordinate if the general did not like the tone of his response.

"Have him survey my treasures and report back to me, and ONLY me, understand?"

"Yes, Sire."

Titus retired to his well-appointed private quarters where he laid down on expensive cushions. His entourage immediately rushed to his side, voluptuous servants bringing him food and wine. Titus did not believe in unnecessary hardships when he was away from Rome. He had brought the finest comforts Rome had to offer. This included his personal staff, who were not soldiers, but servants that he had at home.

After another night of decadence while the population of Jerusalem was starved, petrified or lying dead, Titus was anxious to hear about his haul of stolen treasures. He didn't have to wait too long.

Early the next morning, his rest was interrupted by his Adjutant who appeared at the entrance banging his sword on his shield to announce his presence. "General, your goldsmith is ready to report to you," he announced loudly.

Titus rose and crossed his living area to return to the room where his booty was stored. As he entered this room, his goldsmith stood, a timid fearful looking Jew, pressed into service by his Roman masters.

"Have you finished your report, Jew?"

The frightened slave just nodded his head.

General Titus ordered, "Everyone else OUT!"

He waited for everyone to leave then turned to the slave. "Tell me, Jew, how much gold did I get?"

The frightened man trembled hesitant to give his report.

"Out with it! Hurry up! Tell me about my gold."

"They are all fakes, General; they are all duplicates, gold-plated duplicates of the originals."

Titus was dumbfounded. In a lower voice, lest others hear of his failure, he said, "Show me."

The slave led Titus over to the candlestick and scraped a little gold off to reveal the lead covered structure beneath. He then went to the shewbread and repeated the process. As he worked, he said to the general, "Worthless replicas, all of them."

General Titus' face turned crimson, his body betrayed his great disappointment. In utter confusion, he turned to the slave. "There must be some mistake; this was meant to be my moment of glory. Rome would be so incredulous of the treasures I brought back that they would have no option but to crown me Caesar."

Then in a much lower voice to the man, "Who else knows of this deception, slave?"

"No one, My General. I followed your orders precisely. No one was in the room when I did my work."

General Titus paced the room, thinking, scheming, then nodding as if he had made a decision. Then he asked the slave, "Who ordered the duplicates be made?"

The man trembled again in fear. "The Rabbi Hilal. He removed the originals weeks ago."

Titus walked behind the attentive slave and, in one swift movement, drew his sword and struck a lethal blow to his back. He then walked over to the sack of incense cups, took one and threw it over onto the slave's body.

The general, satisfied with his deception, shouted out, "Guard! Guard!"

The type of shout Titus made brought an immediate reaction; his adjutant and a troop of soldiers came rushing in, swords at the ready, as if the very life of Titus was threatened. He stood tall, pointing to the slave and cup, "Get rid of this body! This slave tried to steal from me."

Titus looked over to his adjutant. "Flavius, put a 24-hour guard on my gold. I don't want anyone else trying to steal this from me. I want every goldsmith in Jerusalem arrested and crucified, displayed on the road east of town.

"This slave told me that the Rabbi Hilal masterminded a deception to hide many other pieces of treasure," he said. "They have been hidden some place outside of the Temple. I want him arrested and brought to me, but do not kill him....yet."

Titus solemnly marched out.

MAKING A PLAN

Thanoon and Hilal were still motionless, if truth be known, they were too shocked to move or even think about their next step. They both looked positively sickly; the atrocities they had watched beyond what the human mind could fathom.

Eventually, Thanoon recovered from his stupor and looked over at his nephew. "Hilal, it is too dangerous to go into Jerusalem tonight, and it is too dangerous to make camp here. Let us go back to the mountains and try to find a safer place to camp."

Hilal looked at his uncle, reality slowly seeping back into his subconscious. He reined his camel around, and they both hurried their mounts away from the sickening scene of human debauchery. After many more hours in the saddle, they found a partially secluded refuge in a rocky ravine. They looked over the area to be sure it was safe enough to make camp.

Once they decided that it would do and had the added benefit that the reek of rotten corpses had disappeared, they unloaded their camels in silence.

Thanoon started to make a small fire to brew some tea. When the water was hot, they drank their tea quietly. After what they had seen that day, there was little to say. Once they finished their tea, they set up camp, wandering around almost like zombies. Dusk turned to night, and they sat down to a dinner of bread and cheese they had brought from Wadi Zuballa.

Both had little appetite, and Hilal was the first to finally speak. "I did not recognize the Old Judea or the glorious suburbs; every trace of beauty has been blotted out by war and cruelty," he lamented.

"Yes, I agree, My Nephew. It is too dangerous for us to go into the city."

Thanoon was now trying to think strategically, but Hilal would have none of it. "I must go, Uncle. The scrolls are too important. I have people waiting for me; my neighbor Mary and a Member of the Way are in Jerusalem putting their lives at risk. I must go, they will help us."

Thanoon had not heard this term before; he asked Hilal with a puzzled look on his face, "What is a Member of the Way?"

"We are the Chosen, to teach and lead others in the way of Jesus."

"Could I become a Member of the Way?" asked Thanoon.

Hilal turned to look long and hard at his uncle. "Let me sleep on this. We will discuss this in the morning." After a moment, he had another thought. "Are you armed?"

Thanoon pulled back his shirt to expose a wide leather sash, slung from one shoulder to the other side of his abdomen, filled with throwing knives. He smiled widely. "If anyone tried to harm us, they would regret it."

"I am going to put my bed close to the fire and then sleep back with our camels," Hilal said.

"You have learned well, Nephew. Good night."

Later, Hilal woke to the noise of a ruckus near the campfire. The night was black as pitch with no light from the moon. He could hear the voice of his uncle, shouting and pleading loudly. It sounded as if he were in trouble, but in his sleepy state, Hilal wondered who could have found them there.

"You don't need that! What do you want?" shouted Thanoon.

Hilal was instantly on alert. He wiped the sleep out of eyes, got up from his hidden sleeping mat, and started toward the noise. He crept stealthily forward. Three unshaven, shaggy barbarians were holding Thanoon. One held his neck while the other two held his arms. A fourth bandit sat on a tree stump and a fifth advanced toward Thanoon with a red-hot, smoldering branch from the fire.

The fourth bandit asked from his tree stump, "Are you going to tell us what we want to know?"

Hilal could tell the fourth bandit was the boss, but his first priority was to deal with the thug advancing toward Thanoon.

Thanoon sounded very worried, shouting louder than necessary, hoping he was being heard by Hilal. "I don't have a stash of cash; I am but a simple Bedouin trader."

The fourth bandit didn't believe him, almost laughing at his response, "I have never heard of a poor Bedouin trader that didn't have any money to trade with. Tell us where your money is and we won't burn your eyes out."

The fifth bandit was a wretched-looking, short, filthy individual with shaggy brown hair and an evil look on his bearded face. He slithered closer to Thanoon, blowing on the glowing branch till it was bright red. Hilal was ready for him. He had crept up and hidden in the bushes so that he was behind Thanoon but in front of the fifth bandit.

The fifth bandit shouted out to his mates, "Oh, I think it's ready now! Let me take his eyes out; I want to hear 'em sizzle!"

In the shadows behind Thanoon and his captors, a branch shook and a shadow passed behind them, gone before they could see what it was.

The fourth bandit, still sitting on the tree stump, shouted out, "'Ere! What the heck was that? Anybody see..." He stopped talking, abruptly standing up to look around. His eyes settled on the fifth bandit who, up until the second before was advancing on Thanoon with the burning branch. His mate had dropped his branch and was staggering backwards, falling on his back into the fire. He was gurgling as his neck and head burnt in the hot embers, clutching at something in his throat.

The fourth bandit went over to his friend to see a knife protruding from the man's windpipe, bleeding profusely. "He's got a knife in his throat! He's done for! Anybody see where it came from? Must be..."

As he shouted, Hilal went around to the other side of the camp, behind him. In a flash, the scribe threw another knife, and it lodged in the eye of the bandit holding Thanoon's neck. He dropped dead, never knowing what hit him.

The other two bandits who were holding Thanoon reduced their grip enough so that he was able to wrestle free. To the surprise of his captors, he swiveled back to them with a knife in each hand.

The second bandit said in a panic, "Where did he get that kni—" He couldn't finish the sentence; he dropped dead as Thanoon cut his jugular.

The first bandit started walking backward, only to run into Hilal, who cut his throat. The fourth bandit looked incredulously at the two men, once his prisoners, now his captors. Before him stood a Bedouin and a rabbi.

He started retreating, begging for his life, "I meant nothing. We were never going to hurt you. It was ... you know ... just a bit of fun."

Thanoon was furious. "Where did you come from?"

The fourth bandit began to shake in fear. "We were just trying to make a living."

Hilal drew another knife and threw it, striking his forehead. He dropped dead.

The scribe, too, was furious, almost out of control. His pent-up anger after seeing the tremendous cruelty inflicted on the people of Jerusalem and then this attack unleashed a primitive part of his being.

"You won't be killing anymore innocents, ever," he spat vehemently.

INTO THE BELLY OF THE BEAST

When daylight broke over the ravine where Thanoon and Hilal had camped, the atmosphere still seemed charged with a palpable sense of foreboding. It was as if the murderous intentions of the invading Roman Army made up a fog, a thick obnoxious, polluted fog bank that expanded ever outward from Jerusalem. This thick haze of evil seemed to have a life of its own, moving by itself and injecting everyone it came across with its own infectious disease.

It was unshakeable, the sense of an impending catastrophe, and so great that it penetrated the soul as it spread across the land. The certainty of extermination could be felt in one's heart, making it simply agonizing to breathe and tormenting the emotional being of all within its boundaries.

When Hilal awoke, Thanoon was crouched over stoking the embers of the campfire. He looked up as Hilal approached, "Good morning, Nephew, can you feel it?"

Hilal knew instantly what he was talking about – the blatant feeling of uneasiness had affected them both.

"Yes, I can. What happened to the bandits? I don't see any of the bodies."

Thanoon answered without looking up. "El Deloua and I took them away last night."

Hilal noticed Thanoon acted differently, his demeanor changed. Gone was the carefree uncle, and Hilal could not put his finger on it exactly, but it was strange.

"We have much to discuss. While you make tea, I want to check out around the camp for tracks or any signs of danger," Thanoon announced without an explanation.

He left the relative safety of their camp with El Deloua. Hilal could see him dismount in the distance, walking along with his head facing down, examining the ground. After some time, he remounted El Deloua and continued his search, looking at the ground.

Later, Thanoon returned to camp, and Hilal could tell that something was preoccupying him. As he came to the small campfire, he told his nephew, "Hilal I do not understand what is happening. Everybody seems to be going mad, stealing from and killing each other."

Hilal found the predicament of the Judeans difficult to understand, as well. After much thought, he answered Thanoon, "Uncle, have you heard of the expression, 'All roads lead to Rome'?"

Thanoon nodded. "Of course. I am not an ignorant Bedouin. All the roads are Roman, where else would they lead?"

Hilal smiled, shaking his head, happy to have his uncle at his side with his straight-forward, honest mannerisms. He thought to himself that there was no subterfuge in this man.

"Tell me what it is you want, I will get it for you," Thanoon said.

Hilal felt the magnitude of his responsibility. He was in deep thought; it was one thing for destiny to call him to risk his life, but he was struggling within himself, wondering whether he could, in good conscience, ask the same of Thanoon. If he chose to tell his uncle about the enormity of the destiny that had been thrust on him, the risk of a tortuous death could be the consequence for both. The danger was very real if he continued to help Hilal.

Finally he decided that his uncle had already made the decision for him; he would not be put off, or sent away. "Uncle, the story I am about to tell you is of such magnitude, the very knowledge of it could result in you being tortured and crucified."

Hilal watched Thanoon as his bearing completely changed. He was suddenly all ears, wanting to know and would not accept being led blindly into danger. He had to know the truth; he demanded to know it.

"Uncle, once I tell you this story, my destiny becomes yours. If I don't live to fulfill my mission, you must fulfill it for me."

Thanoon had his most sincere look as he waited for Hilal to begin, acknowledging that this was only to be expected. Instead of answering that way, he explained his feelings. "A long time ago, I followed a little boy into the desert. He was on a quest; his destiny was calling him. I saw a little boy grow into a man on that lonely trip."

Hilal remembered his trip to his father's camp. "My life has been dedicated to you ever since that day," Thanoon said. "Did you know I followed you that night? When you went to find your father to ask his blessing to follow your destiny?"

"It seems so long ago, but no, I did not know you followed me."

Thanoon was close to choking up at the emotional memory of it all. "Your mother asked me to, when she came clamoring into my tent that night you ran off."

Hilal smiled in retrospect, turning his head side to side. Thanoon interrupted his melancholy recollections, "Hilal, I'm sorry. Continue with your story."

"The Romans want to destroy the second Temple in Jerusalem. For many years, the Temple served as the State Treasury and the archive for the scrolls, the recorded history of Judaism. The riches inside Temple Mount were beyond compare."

Thanoon was obviously paying attention. "You said 'were,' Nephew, not 'are.' Why?"

Hilal was glad to see his uncle picked up on the inconsistency. "I will get to that in a moment. When Moses came down from Mount Sinai, he had with him instructions to build a giant, golden candelabra. When he got back to Jerusalem, together with some of the best goldsmiths in town, he commissioned a candlestick of pure gold to be made. His instructions were precise. It would be made of seven branches. The base, the branches, and all the flowers on the branches were of pure gold."

"Why seven branches?"

"They stood for the seven days of the creation."

Thanoon was totally absorbed in the story. "You didn't steal the candlestick did you?"

"Uncle, be serious. No, I didn't steal it, but we also did not want the Romans to steal it. That, as well as the other artifacts, are too important and mean too much to the Jewish people. To let the Romans steal those artifacts would be another atrocity."

"So what did you do? I am fascinated with this story."

"This war and the siege of Jerusalem have been going on for nearly four years. When it became evident that the Romans wanted to destroy Jerusalem, we developed a plan."

Thanoon leaned in, clearly anticipating every word. "You are full of surprises, Nephew. So what sneakiness have you been up to? What did you plan to do?"

"We employed several goldsmiths, sworn to secrecy. These volunteers, who knew the danger they faced, were charged with making exact duplicates of the artifacts out of lead, then gold-plating them all."

Thanoon laughed hysterically. He couldn't control his guffaws of merriment. Hilal continued his story. "These goldsmiths created the duplicates, then set about dismantling the real relics into smaller pieces so I could smuggle them out of Temple Mount under the very noses of the Romans."

"My Nephew, you are unbelievable! Who came up with this plot?"

"I did."

As soon as Thanoon stopped laughing, his subconscious returned him to reality, and he felt a sense of foreboding; they needed to leave this place.

"It is time to move from here; let's break camp, and we can continue our conversation."

In the distance, smoke rose from Jerusalem. Overhead, the circling vultures began to descend for their morning feast on the rotting corpses.

This sharing of stories had done much to lift their spirits and they both felt as if a load had been lifted from them, leaving them rejuvenated. The mood as they broke camp was in stark contrast to the one they had been in when they arrived.

After finishing their preparations, the pair resumed their travel toward Jerusalem. The ferocious atrocities of the previous day were over. Hilal and Thanoon could now see to the east of the city, on the Mount of Olives, a Roman Legion of more than 5,000 infantry were camped. Smoke rose from numerous campfires, and the noise of soldiers practicing their swordsmanship was audible even from afar.

To the west, on Mount Scopus, an even larger army was camped. The flag of the Roman General Titus flew over all of the encampments. Another legion of Roman soldiers waited, camped on the outskirts of Jerusalem, held in reserve.

"This is the most incredible assembly of an army I have ever seen. We are going to have to be very careful," Thanoon said.

HILAL, HUNTED

Hilal and Thanoon approached Jerusalem. In the distance they saw the East Gate.

"Who is the disciple we are meeting in Jerusalem?" Thanoon asked.

Hilal thought his answer would surprise his uncle, and it did, "Jude."

"Do you mean the boy from our village who used to bully you?"

"The same."

"But how did that happen? Him I have got to see!"

"He came to me some years back, his life was in turmoil. His family had died, and he wanted to make up for his cruelty as a boy. He asked for my forgiveness," Hilal said. "He has proven himself --just an ordinary man with extraordinary courage. He is waiting for us with my neighbor, Mary."

Then looking seriously at his uncle, Hilal added, "She is much prettier than El Deloua!" He laughed. "Thanoon, on a more serious subject, the Romans will be watching my house. When we arrive, we will have little time and I will have to leave as soon as they spot me.

"You must stay and help Jude and Mary load the camels," Hilal said. "Then you can catch up to me. I will go toward Aqaba from the South Gate.

"Where did you hide everything?"

"Underneath my home in Jerusalem. You will find a wooden trap door three inches beneath the floor. All of the Scrolls are hidden there, the treasures as well. Leave the treasures, but load the scrolls to take to the caves."

"Uncle, the time has come; we must split up. I will go on foot to my home. Leave my camel tied up at the South Gate. As soon as the Romans leave my neighborhood, load the camels and help Jude and Mary escape."

Thanoon felt the weight of his responsibility – to be loyal to Hilal, he had to help him with the scrolls, but to be loyal to his sister and brother-in-law, he should stay with Hilal and protect him.

He decided that loyalty to his sister and her husband was tantamount, and declared to Hilal, defiantly, "I will not leave you!"

Hilal was also sure of where his loyalties lay and that at this moment, the history of a people was more important than his life. Equally defiant, he told Thanoon, "You must! If anything happens to me, take the scrolls and my body to Qumran. I'll show you what to do."

Thanoon did a double take, shaking his head, "But if you are dead …?"

He did not understand, but he did believe in his nephew. He thought to himself about the story Hilal told him about Jesus waking the dead. Perhaps that could happen to Hilal.

He didn't get to finish his thoughts; Hilal had spotted danger. It was time, he told Thanoon. "Now go, Uncle! We are in danger together. Remember, I love you as if you were my own father."

Thanoon turned to leave; it was a very emotional moment for him. He had never had children nor even taken a wife. The emotions he felt were a strange development for him and much different than the sentiment he held for El Deloua. With a shaky voice he replied, "Blessings, my son."

"Blessings, my father."

Hilal dismounted, giving his camel to Thanoon. Roman soldiers were everywhere, more intent on harassing people trying to leave town than those entering. General Titus had given his orders – "'No Quarter,' kill them all; man, woman or child, civilian or fighter, kill them." The only ones to receive a pass were the workers who supplied provisions to the invading Romans.

Hilal walked stealthily toward his house, moving in the shadows. Fortunately for him, he had lived in Jerusalem for so long he knew all the back alleys and secret passages through the markets and public areas. As he reached his own neighborhood, he saw off to one side his neighbor's house. From within, Mary and Jude were watching.

His attention was drawn to some movement across the street – Roman spies or troops, hidden, waiting for him to appear. Hilal ran to a spot on a corner and looked over some stalls near his house. Again creeping forward, he risked a peek out around the corner then he stuck his head out.

A Roman soldier spotted him and he shouted to his comrades, "There he is! Get him! Remember, we must catch him alive! General Titus will disembowel anyone who injures him."

Hilal took off running. He could hear Roman troops behind him, alerted and moving to take up the chase. The ominous sound of marching leather boots on pavement, swords banging against shields, drifted toward him – soldiers at double-march, giving chase. The alleys of Jerusalem were not like Roman roads; they twisted and turned, leading into crowded areas and were not conducive to marching in formation.

Hilal looked around and ran fast, seeing soldiers following. As the Roman soldiers saw him, they broke formation and sprinted toward him, pushing people to the ground.

One of the pursuing Roman soldiers shouted to those in front of him, "Make way you fools! Make way! Get out of our way or suffer the consequences!"

People scattered all over the place as soldiers ran through a market full of vendors, some displaying the few goods they had, many stalls empty. Hilal ducked into another alley and through a market running faster and faster.

The soldiers lost sight of him, and he completed his planned circle back to his neighborhood. Roman soldiers were still everywhere.

He heard a Roman officer ordering his underlings, "Alert all sentries in case he tries to leave the city. Send a platoon to each gate."

As the officer made his order, hundreds of soldiers arrived in Hilal's neighborhood. The platoons of marching soldiers trotted off for the North, South, East and West gates of the city.

Hilal took off again for the South Gate. Before long, he was spotted. "There he goes! Make way!" shouted another soldier.

Two more soldiers ran after Hilal, and he ducked into a synagogue. The soldiers hesitated, trying to see where he went, while Hilal ran out the far side. The soldiers lost sight of him again. He needed the break; winded, he slowed down and put a cloth over his head as he walked along the street, trying to act an innocent spectator. He heard the sound of a Roman Platoon trotting behind him trying to catch up.

At the sound of the approaching platoon, the South Gate came into sight, and he hurried in a last-ditch effort to reach the exit before the platoon got there to secure it. He saw his camel tied nearby, watched by a boy outside the gate. He reached the gate and ran through, grabbing the reins on the fly. The boy was scared half to death, and ran away, disappearing into the underworld of town.

The soldiers finally arrived behind Hilal and gave chase on foot, but he was now at a full gallop taking off for the desert. He ran his camel at the fastest gait it could manage, directing his mount through gullies, into a wadi, and then up the other side over a dune toward some mountains.

He looked behind him to find Roman soldiers assembling at the South Gate and platoon after platoon taking off in his direction. The Romans were now after him, in formation, double-marching across the rough terrain fearlessly. He ran scared at the sight of soldiers coming relentlessly after him.

Silently, he prayed that he had given enough time for Thanoon to get Jude and Mary loaded and on their way to Qumran.

SECRETING AWAY THE SCROLLS

Thanoon watched Hilal's neighborhood, it seemed the Roman soldiers had gone. He kept scanning the streets, thinking it was clear. Finally, he walked over to Mary's house leading ten camels.

As he approached, the door opened and a head popped out cautiously. "You must be Thanoon? I am Mary."

He saw the prettiest green eyes he had ever gazed upon, and asked her, "Do you have the scrolls ready to move?"

Mary walked out so Thanoon could see her, and his eyes lingered. She brought him back to the present by saying, "We are ready."

"Hilal has bought us some time," he answered quietly.

Thanoon went into the house to help bring out all of the bags and containers. He, Mary and Jude hitched the handles over the camels' saddles, making one trip at a time until they were ready to go. They headed for the East Gate. Travel to the gate was relatively easy, since all of the Roman foot soldiers in town had been deployed to the South Gate to search for Hilal. His diversion had worked.

JERUSALEM'S EAST GATE

As Thanoon, Mary and Jude arrived at the gate, Roman soldiers were still patrolling. Word must have been received that the manhunt for Hilal was now concentrated on the South Gate, as the guards were more relaxed here.

Thanoon handed Jude the leather map of the Qumran caves, telling him, "Go now. I must go help Hilal. If you follow these directions, you will find the cave. If you see a thorn bush, you will be close. Now go! Wait for us there."

With a flourish and a last glance at Mary, Thanoon was gone, leaving Mary and Jude alone. Jude led the team of camels on toward the gate. As they did so, a Roman soldier approached, "Halt! Why so many camels?"

Jude answered for them. "My wife is with child. We are leaving Jerusalem to go to Jericho. Jerusalem is no place for a child to be born."

The soldier started to walk around the camels, and as he did so, Jude said, "After I take my wife to Jericho, I have been ordered to go to Alexandria to pick up supplies for Titus – oil, corn and wine for your soldiers."

The soldier stood aside then. "Hurry on back with some wine for me, go. Go."

Jude and Mary took off, leading their camels silently into the desert for the road to the Dead Sea. Mary looked over at Jude when they were out of earshot of the Roman guard. "That was very clever of you, Jude," she said. "Hilal will be very proud of you. But I am glad they didn't think to check my belly."

"Me, too," he said.

JERUSALEM SOUTH GATE

Thanoon made the trip back to the South Gate in record time. As he approached, he noticed all the frantic activity of the Roman soldiers rushing off into the desert, and he decided to watch, mounted on El Deloua. It was not a wise move, he would admit in retrospect.

As he watched the Romans, more troops of Centurions in front prepared to chase Hilal. Thanoon was too relaxed and kept asking himself which direction Hilal had taken.

He was so immersed in his own thoughts that he did not notice another troop of Romans approaching from behind, led by a Roman captain. As Thanoon watched, the platoon in front took off toward the mountains. Ever the smart Alec, Thanoon burst out laughing, slapping his leg in merriment, "Oh, El Deloua, only the Romans would take off into the desert with so little water."

He thought himself so funny that he guffawed loudly and didn't notice Captain Octavius and his Roman troops behind him …that is until he heard the scrape of a sword being withdrawn from its scabbard and pummeled on a shield.

Octavius was not amused. He demanded to know, "What is so amusing?"

Thanoon was taken totally by surprise; he had not expected anyone to bother with him. But he answered truthfully, "I was watching that platoon leave at a trot under the midday sun, and I thought it funny that they did not carry any water."

The Roman captain did not think this funny at all. He turned to the soldiers under his command and ordered, "Seize him!"

As soon as Thanoon realized the predicament he was in, he kicked El Deloua in the flanks with all his might, hoping she would jump forward. The Roman captain was too quick for him, slashing with his heavy sword at Thanoon. Luckily, he missed and instead sliced open a gash on El Deloua's rump as she jumped sideways.

Thanoon was not expecting the move sideways instead of forward. He lost his balance, fell to the ground, and before he could rise to defend himself, five Roman soldiers were on top of him.

El Deloua was frightened. She had unexpectedly unseated her master and was limping badly. She still had her wits about her because she kept running out of reach of the Romans; she would run as the enemy approached, then just stand still, watching.

The five Roman soldiers on top of Thanoon were too much for him, and he could hardly breathe let alone push them off. The soldiers got up slowly, hanging onto their prize as if he were gold. Carefully, they bound his feet, then his hands. Only when he was immobilized did they relax their grip somewhat.

Thanoon was forced to the ground again, sitting hunched over as his Roman captors surveyed him. A feeling of total helplessness flooded him and he sat looking up at the Romans, knowing that they could cut off his head just as easily as release him.

Octavius watched the proceedings, silently. After Thanoon was hog-tied, he ordered his men, "Go capture that camel; should be worth something."

Four Romans walked off toward El Deloua, hands extended as if to offer her a treat. As soon as they got close, she ran off. She retreated a good distance away then turned to watch her antagonists. As they approached again, she ran off, only to turn and watch them again. Frustrated, this time they charged her, swords drawn. She easily outran them then turned to watch. The Roman captain was getting embarrassed by his troop's performance, his body language evidencing his aggravation. In desperation, he waved them back to camp.

"You men cannot even capture a defenseless camel!" he bellowed, turning around and walking off a little distance.

The soldiers returned to their comrades, hunching their shoulders, as if to say, 'Stupid camel.'

"Let's make camp here; bring that prisoner over." The captain ordered from where he had walked.

The Roman guards brought Thanoon to Octavius and set him down. The captain looked Thanoon over and said, "So you think Roman soldiers are funny?"

Thanoon wisely chose not to answer. He watched and waited. One of the troopers asked, "Captain, what are we going to do with the prisoner? Do you want to let him go?"

Octavius had been thinking about that. "No, I have a better solution. The Fifth Legion is going to take a detachment of Christian prisoners to the Amphitheater in Caesarea for the games. Let's send him there."

IN THE HANDS OF ROMANS

JERUSALEM - THE FOLLOWING MORNING

The days following the Romans' final assault on the Temple were just as horrific as those before. What remained of the Temple was set on fire, and anyone they found was slaughtered. Women and children had hidden themselves in various chambers, and these, too, were set ablaze. The Romans' blood thirst was unquenchable, and the fires raged for hours. The Temple was burned to the ground as the prophecy of Jesus – not one stone left upon another – was fulfilled.

Once the Temple was leveled, the Romans swept down into the Lower City to wreak their vengeance and hatred on that that part of Jerusalem. The result left Jerusalem a wasteland. Everyone despaired.

General Titus ordered every goldsmith in town to be crucified as a punishment for the deception engineered by Hilal. These orders fell on the shoulders of Octavius, the Roman captain. He knew how desperate the survivors of Jerusalem were.

He went to the center of the city, stood tall on a well, and shouted out a proclamation to the people.

"I need ten men for a day's work – three loaves of bread and three dinar for each worker."

That was an absolute fortune in devastated Jerusalem, and immediately he had ten volunteers.

"After you have filled your belly, I want you to go around the city announcing a new program for metal workers. You will shout, 'The Roman Army has work for silversmiths and goldsmiths – three loaves of bread and three dinar per day.' Tell them to come to our command center."

Octavius' plan went off without a hitch, and almost before he got back to his command post, a line of metal workers was forming. After an hour, he had his forty-four straggly, starving workers lining up looking for their share of offered wages and food. The reception was not quite what they had expected. They were led off to an area where they could not be seen, tied up, and then questioned. After all the hardships these people had already suffered, they were tortured unmercifully.

The only real question the Romans wanted answered was who was responsible for organizing the plan to hide the gold and other wealth from the Temple. The first slave tied to a tree was asked, "Who employed you at the Temple?"

A very simple question, but the slave refused to answer. The Roman in charge was a bloodthirsty bully named Brutus. He asked the slave again, "Are you sure you won't answer my question?"

The slave just nodded in the affirmative. Brutus was hoping for this result; he wanted an excuse to intimidate and frighten the rest of the goldsmiths. He called over an accomplice, stood in front of this slave, and growled, "Well, Slave, as you are not willing to talk, you won't be needing your tongue anymore, will you?"

The slave's reaction was immediate; he replied to Brutus in a terrified, weak voice, "I'll tell you! It was Rabbi Hilal. I swear it was him."

Brutus acknowledged the response calmly, then turned to his accomplice and shouted, "Soldier, remove his tongue!"

One soldier gripped the poor man's face and forced his mouth open, while a second poked blacksmith's tongs into the man's mouth, secured his tongue and forcibly pulled it out. The soldier holding his face sliced off the appendage.

Forty-three goldsmiths simultaneously started praying, some wetting themselves in fear, but they all realized one irrefutable fact – this was their last day on earth.

After they all had confirmed that Rabbi Hilal was the ringleader of the deception, they were led away to be crucified. His mission completed, Octavius returned to General Titus' command center to report to Flavius.

"Captain, I believe you have had some success in your mission?" asked the Adjutant Flavius.

Octavius stood proudly at attention. "Yes, Sir. One goldsmith revealed that there was a secret council of rabbis charged with protecting Temple treasures. The ringleader was a rabbi named Hilal."

Flavius was very pleased. "I am appointing you to General Titus' staff as my personal aide, Captain." Then he added, "Did you find out anything else from the gold and silver smiths?

The Roman captain beamed with pride at his new appointment. He responded, "Just that this goldsmith thought the treasures were still in Jerusalem."

THE ROAD TO CAESAREA FROM JERUSALEM

A detachment from Octavius' troop took Thanoon over to one of the departure points for the Fifth Legion taking prisoners to Caesarea. Thanoon had only contempt for these heathens. His initial reaction had been to rebel at any chance he had, but after seeing the inhumane cruelty with which the prisoners were treated, he decided to swallow his pride and act more demurely.

He didn't want to attract the attention of the guards with the painful whips. Anyone thought to be too weak to make the journey was immediately executed. Thanoon grasped the reality of the situation; resistance was futile at the moment. He would have to bide his time. Roman soldiers rounded up the rest of those still able to walk, taking them over to the blacksmiths where they were to be chained for the long walk to Caesarea.

Roman prison guards were some of the most depraved, bloodthirsty monsters in the entire Roman Army. That was why they had been assigned to look after prisoners. Accustomed to inhumanity, they inflicted punishment with hate and impunity. Armed with 6 foot whips, they patrolled up and down the lines of prisoners, peeling the skin from the back of any victim who didn't obey orders immediately.

After a slight delay, they were told to stand ready to march. Among this crowd, Thanoon stood still relatively strong. Off in the distance, a lone camel watched. El Deloua had followed her master. A crack of the whip signaled the prisoners to start their walk to Caesarea.

The guard shouted, "March, you Christian dogs! March!"

That first day, many of the weak dropped to the ground, their comrades too feeble to help, and the guards executed them where they fell. Thanoon thought that for many of the prisoners, it was a blessing; they were being released from their sufferings. As the slaves were beaten, whipped or died, in the distance, El Deloua watched, following the prisoners – following her master.

One prisoner close to Thanoon had noticed the camel following them, and saw Thanoon looking back frequently at the animal. This prisoner couldn't restrain his curiosity any longer. "Why do you keep looking behind us? Are you watching that camel?"

Thanoon was just too proud of El Deloua to deny her to this new friend. He answered very proudly, "That is not just any camel. That is my El Deloua."

The Jewish prisoner was quiet; he did not know quite what to think about a Bedouin prisoner who expressed such devotion to a camel. The forced-march was in fact taking so much out of them physically that it was a relief not too talk. Later that night, after a long day, the prisoners were told to stop and rest, but no food or water was spared for them.

THE DESERT OUTSIDE THE SOUTH GATE

Hilal felt uneasy and his sleep was spotty at best. He had not prepared for a night spent out in the open and he was too concerned to light a fire. The cold desert air on an unsheltered mesa without good cover meant a very restless night. He was glad to finally see the sun come up from the East.

As he rose, he looked around to see if he could find any kindling, debating with himself about whether he should start a fire to brew some water. He stretched and walked over to the edge of the Mesa, looking down the mountain toward Jerusalem.

Abruptly, his stretch and the massaging of his lower back were interrupted in mid-stroke. He stopped, seeing beneath him a platoon of Roman soldiers camped. They had moved up during the night.

Hilal ran in a panic to the other side of his Mesa, where another platoon was camped. Another dash to the other side found more Romans. He was completely surrounded.

He went back to his camp, close to the first sighting of the Romans. He peeked over again and saw activity below him. A lookout had spotted Hilal, and the Roman in charge had been notified that Hilal was moving around the top of the Mesa.

The Roman officer walked as close as he could get, formed his hands as if imitating a bull horn and shouted up to him, "Rabbi Hilal, you are completely surrounded. Do you want us to come up and get you or will you come down?"

Hilal was devastated, after a long pause to look around, he stopped and thought his situation through. He decided he had no options; he just hoped he had given Thanoon enough time to get the scrolls, Mary and Jude to safety.

"I will come down."

He returned to his camp, dejected, his dreams looking doubtful. Perhaps he would never make it back to Wadi Zuballa to join the Council of Elders. He knelt down, looked up, and prayed out loud. "Please, God, give me the strength to endure and the wisdom to safeguard our scrolls."

With that simple prayer, Hilal started his walk down the hill to surrender to the waiting Romans.

GENERAL TITUS' CAMP

Word had spread like wildfire that Rabbi Hilal had been caught, and Roman soldiers lined the road as he was led shackled to General Titus' camp on the Mount of Olives. Many threw dung at him, but they had to be careful lest they hit one of their own.

After a tortuous walk through the soldiers' camp, he was led directly to Flavius at the command post. Adjutant Flavius was smiling, almost licking his chops in anticipation as Hilal approached. He threw the flap back on his command post tent to reveal an eight foot tripod suspended close to a small fire.

Hilal had been brutally manhandled. By now, he was filthy, muddy and carrying his fair share of whatever refuse the crowd had thrown at him. He was then shoved over to the tripod and secured by his feet. As soon as his feet were tied, a rope was secured to the top of the tripod, inserted into a pulley, and he was pulled upside down until he was vertical. He was then stripped down to his loin cloth. Immediately, two of the notorious prison guards entered with their whips handy.

It was fortunate that everyone was under orders not to kill or permanently maim him or they would have swung him over the small fire that burned close by. The two guards proceeded to take turns striking his back with their whips. After he had endured the typical Roman idea of softening up a prisoner, Flavius re-entered, looked over Hilal's torso and smiled with pleasure.

He was not a genteel man on his best of days. In a mocking, sneering manner he asked Hilal, "Are you going to tell me where the gold is?"

Hilal might have been softened up physically, but spiritually he was as dedicated as ever. He spat out to Flavius, surprising the officer with his strength and vigor, "You arrogant heathen, it is not your gold! You are nothing but a bunch of corrupt, murderous thieves!"

Hilal saw that his outburst had the desired effect as Flavius seethed, unbelieving that this prisoner would be so fool-hardy as to say that to him. He was close to losing control, but reined himself in only because he was under orders not to kill this Jew until he had the information that Titus wanted.

He shouted angrily, "Our spies tell us that you were the ringleader of the rabbis that stole the gold from the Temple!"

Hilal did not respond. Flavius turned to a soldier and ordered him, "Guard, twenty lashes. Don't spare him!"

Hilal contorted with pain as each blow struck and he swung in that direction, almost adding dizziness to his troubles. He was still not beaten, and through clenched teeth he said to Flavius, "How does one steal what is ours? You are the thieves. You will get no treasure from the Temple."

Flavius had a masochistic streak; he enjoyed inflicting pain on others. For him, watching his guards whip Hilal was almost more pleasure than he could bear. He expected some more resistance, so he took great pleasure in telling Hilal, "We have already recovered the Menorah, the shrew table and many other smaller pieces. We are just looking for the other golden treasures that you have hidden."

It was not Hilal who was in for a surprise. He laughed painfully at Flavius, further infuriating him. Flavius thought this was the most prideful soul he had ever met. He was going to take great pleasure in causing Hilal the most painful death possible.

At the moment Flavius thought about Hilal's painful demise, Hilal thought about how he would enjoy the reaction he saw when he told Flavius about the counterfeit relics.

"You have nothing! All you have are gold-plated, worthless duplicates that we left for you buffoons!"

Flavius' face fell to the floor, he was so taken aback. He hissed back at Hilal, "What do you mean, duplicates?"

Hilal was in great pain from the whipping but still managed to get great satisfaction as he spit out his next words with volumes of venom. "The treasure you 'stole' is worthless. All fakes. You can carry it all back to your heathen emperor as a tribute to your spectacular failure to conquer God's chosen people."

Flavius' reaction was even more remarkable than Hilal imagined. He rose up as if growing in stature with his anger and approached the tripod until he swelled over Hilal's swinging body. He was so angry it seemed as if his next words rumbled up from his bowels. "Slave, that talk is blasphemy! You could die for that!"

Hilal was still defiant. "To die is my destiny; others will take over for me. You will follow me shortly, barbarian."

This was more than Flavius could take; he was close to losing control and snarled out his next words. "I am not a barbarian; I am a Roman Centurion."

This time, he did lose control. He rose, withdrew his sword then hesitated. He knew if he harmed Hilal, the consequences to him would be fatal; he was under orders. Instead, he opened the flap of his tent to leave, saying to Hilal, "Let us see if you are still this brave in the morning, Christian."

Flavius turned to the guard whipping Hilal. "Time to leave."

They both left Hilal alone swinging upside down.

THE ROAD TO CAESAREA

TITUS' PRIVATE QUARTERS

Flavius had waited to report to General Titus until he cooled down somewhat. This Hilal was proving to be an enigma; certainly not the cowardly rabbi he had expected. It was time though; Flavius decided. He walked over to Titus' tent, taking deep breaths as he went. By the time he walked into General Titus' private quarters, he was close to being under control.

General Titus nodded to Flavius as he entered. "What progress, Flavius, on the recovery of my gold?" he asked casually.

"I am working on him now; I believe by morning, he will tell me what you want to know. He had the audacity to suggest that the treasures you have already retrieved were fakes."

If Flavius had been a more intuitive man, he would have noticed the reaction from General Titus. Suddenly there was total silence in the tent. The general's demeanor changed, and his face became drawn back tight, as if trying to control himself.

General Titus chose his next words very carefully. "What else did the rabbi say?" he said through clenched teeth.

"Nothing, General."

Flavius was standing at attention, beaming with pride. Titus walked around behind him, stealthily withdrawing his sword. Flavius heard the sound of the sword scraping the sheath as it was withdrawn. Standing at attention, to turn around and look to see what Titus was doing would be unsoldierly, he knew. For the first time in his life, he prayed.

With one violent thrust, Titus pushed the point up through Flavius' heart. He fell to the ground, still praying incoherently, dying. As he fell, General Titus mumbled quietly, "You fool, nobody must know, nobody."

FLAVIUS' COMMAND CENTER

Hilal was still swinging upside down, blood dripping from his wounds. The fire was now a distant memory, only hissing occasionally when a bead of

Hilal's sweat or blood dropped onto some embers buried under the surface ash.

He was near the end, slipping in and out of consciousness and had a hard time differentiating between reality and fantasy. His mind was wandering all through his life. He saw the mysterious stranger in the Temple telling him that his destiny was calling. He went back to the beginning of his journey and was once again at his father's house gathering up skins to take to market.

He heard a faint tearing sound, but did not understand; he was not tearing his skins. He opened his eyes to see a slit being opened in the outside wall of the canvas command center. He closed his eyes, thinking he must be dreaming, but which was the dream? Was he swinging upside down or was he at his father's house?

He heard the strange noise again and looked over to see a knife appear; it was cutting a vertical opening in the side of the tent. He closed his eyes. He was hugging his skins tightly as he walked to market, then the village bully, Jude, appeared, laughing and taunting him, encouraging the village children to rob the skins from his possession. He would never forget that voice – that voice of childhood cruelty.

Then a head appeared; and he heard that voice; he recognized it again. "Oh, my God," he said to himself, "I can't let that bully steal my skins! My whole future depends on it. No! No!"

But he could not escape; his arms tied behind his back. The voice – that voice – was gentle now, a hand stroking his forehead as the voice spoke lovingly to him, "Hilal, my friend… Hilal, it is your friend, Jude. I have come to rescue you."

Hilal still resisted and struggled against his ropes as Jude tried to lovingly revive him. "Hilal, it is Jude. You are dreaming; open your eyes."

As if being pulled back from the very gates of death, Hilal forced open his eyes. He saw Jude – but not the childhood bully, it was the older, wiser Jude, still with one eyeless socket swollen shut, but a Jude with compassion. It was his new friend, the Jude he forgave.

Jude tried to hug his friend, who groaned in pain. Feeling somehow culpable for Hilal's situation, Jude said, "I am so sorry, Hilal, sorry for everything I have done to you."

Hilal was still moaning in agony. Jude put his hands under Hilal's whip-raw back to lift him up as gingerly as possible. While securing Hilal with one hand, Jude reached for the knots holding Hilal's ankles. Painstakingly slowly, he undid them and lay Hilal down.

Only then did Hilal open his eyes, still struggling to differentiate between reality and his dreams. Slowly, the world came into focus, and Hilal saw Jude then he looked around and recognized the command post in which he had been tortured.

His pupils narrowed as he concentrated his focus on Jude. Then it became so confusing again. He managed to squeak out, "Jude, what are you doing here? Are you after my skins?"

Jude knew that Hilal was close to the edge of life and death, walking a fine line between fantasy and reality. He needed to shock Hilal back to the present, and said in a very frightened voice, "I killed the guard, Hilal. I killed a man."

Jude acted as if in a panic, and his shocking confession drew a reaction from Hilal, who whispered back to him, "You killed a man?"

""Yes," responded Jude, adding, "There was a guard in front of your tent; we must hurry."

Hilal was now focusing. He asked Jude, "The scrolls?"

Jude beamed proudly, he had never been so happy to have someone ask him a question because it proved Hilal was back in the land of the living.

"They are safe in Qumran with Mary. Now, I must get you out of here."

Hilal made a miraculous recovery, springing into action. "Go get the guard you killed; bring his body here."

Jude scampered off with his new orders, leaving Hilal to look for water. Outside, Jude found the Roman guard's body as he had left it. He dragged it over to the tent, and with great difficulty, heaved the corpse inside.

Hilal watched Jude struggle with the body, but instead of helping him, he ordered Jude, "Undress him to his loin cloth, then strap him up as I was. We will put the fire under his head so he will be unrecognizable in the morning. Then I will march you out of here, dressed as a soldier."

While Jude began doing as he was bid, Hilal, put more wood from the stack on the fire. After blowing hard enough to get the flames going again, he walked over to the stack of clothes Jude had pulled off the Roman. With much difficulty, Hilal dressed as a guard and with a few final adjustments by Jude, he was ready.

Hilal, the Roman Centurion, rose to his feet, still very wobbly. Jude supported him by the elbow until he could stand on his own.

Then Hilal looked at Jude, who needed little help to look like a wretched prisoner. "Let's go."

Hilal led Jude, the prisoner, out of camp and after a minute they came to their first obstacle. They approached the check point in the darkness, and a Roman soldier barked, "Halt! Who goes there?"

Hilal answered smoothly, "Centurion with a prisoner, on orders of General Titus."

By now the Roman guard could see Hilal and his uniform. "Pass."

ROMAN ROAD TO CAESAREA - THE NEXT DAY

As the sun rose over the eastern horizon, ten miles outside of Jerusalem, bedraggled prisoners laid on the immaculate Roman road leading to Caesarea. They had had no food or water for at least a day. Many did not survive the night or were unable to get up.

The pristine road, made of symmetrical blocks of limestone was in stark contrast to the starving, thirsty, filthy near-death prisoners. Thanoon looked over to the desert behind them to see El Deloua foraging within a 100 yards.

He shouted out gently, hoping not to raise the ire of the prison guards, "El Deloua!"

Hearing her master, she abruptly raised her head, looking straight at Thanoon.

Risking it all, at the top of his voice, he shouted, "Hilal! Hilal!"

El Deloua gave one last glance at Thanoon and trotted off west toward the Dead Sea.

ROMAN ROAD TO CAESAREA 20 MILES OUT - EVENING

Although the Roman guards held their Jewish captives in total disdain, there were limits to their cruelty. If they arrived in Caesarea with only empty shackles, they could well find themselves participating in the games to replace their murdered prisoners.

The second day was even more torturous than the first and many prisoners in the procession were not able to go at the speed that the Roman guards desired. This resulted in the able dragging the tired forward, the chains of the dead clanging loudly along the stone road as more were emptied from their captives.

More than twenty Roman guards made the journey and most were now frustrated by the slow pace of the prisoners, darkening their moods and increasing their anger and brutality to their wards. Finally, the order came for the prisoners to stop and rest. Most dropped where they stopped. Fearing more deaths would seriously deplete the ranks of the contestants for the games, the guards chose to camp underneath the intersection of an aqueduct that delivered fresh water to Caesarea.

Thanoon still seemed to be the strongest prisoner on the chain gang, an asset that was advantageous to him but also made him a target for the dysfunctional, jealous guards.

As he was judged to be strong, a soldier pointed to him and ordered, "You there, climb up to the aqueduct and bring water back down for the prisoners. We camp here tonight."

Thanoon welcomed the chance to be released from his chains and feel the freedom of unrestricted movement. With joy in his heart, he climbed up the stone pillar of the aqueduct to the water. Once free at the highest point in his vicinity, he put his hand to his forehead to scan the terrain all around him. His primary concern was to see if El Deloua was still following. He scanned the horizon, but she was nowhere to be seen.

He filled as many skins as he could, all the while checking the area around him. His travel partner was gone. It has often been said that 'hope springs eternal.' Thanoon, in the darkest hours of his life, suddenly had hope.

He descended the aqueduct with water for all.

QUMRAN CAVES - THE NEXT DAY

Mary had never experienced such solitude. She had tried to stay busy, organizing what she could, cleaning and waiting for her friends. Finally, she decided to go out into the sunlight to see her surroundings.

As she approached the entrance, the light from outside grew in intensity from the gloomy half-light to which she had grown accustomed. She stopped to blow out her oil lamp. There was a small alcove in the wall that Thanoon had cleaned out that she used to store her lamp. As she stretched out to put the lamp away, an unusual sound penetrated the cave. Mary glanced up, trying to place the noise. She was not sure whether to run and hide or leave the cave. She decided to run out, and as she did, she almost ran head-first into Jude, who shouted urgently at her, "Mary, help me! I have Hilal outside; he is unconscious."

Mary was too relieved to see a friend to hear what he had said. She shouted back angrily, "Jude, I wish you wouldn't do that!"

Jude was turning to go back and get Hilal with Mary's help. He looked at her, "what did I do?"

"You crept up on me, you scoundrel! You could have shouted that you were coming."

Jude ignored the comment and they both went to the entrance. He untied Hilal from the camel where he had secured the rabbi's dead weight, as Mary rushed over to help.

She looked over her wounded friend as they carried him quickly into the cave and set him down close to the fire. Then in total shock at his condition, she said, "Good heavens, Jude! Whatever happened to him?"

Hilal lay prone on the floor, face-down as Mary checked his raw back. She rushed off to get towels and ointments to tend to his wounds. Jude sat, resting after his escapade, and watched her work.

"I'm sorry if I scared you back there," he said.

"It is alright. What happened to him?"

'The Romans tortured him," he said, the evidence before them belying the simplicity of that statement.

CAESAREA

Thanoon felt so much better after a night's rest and fresh water. He was as hungry as could be. The wind was blowing in from the coast and he could smell the salty air. He knew that meant his journey would soon be over.

The guards had started the morning as soon as light broke; they wanted to get to their barracks. Thanoon and his bedraggled fellow prisoners shuffled on toward Caesarea. He looked around at the other survivors. The chained slaves had dwindled to less than half. Empty leg and arm shackles drug along the stone road, dragging noisily and reminding them of those who had died on the journey.

Thanoon pretended to be more exhausted than he really was. The other poor wretches had been suffering from malnutrition for weeks as they endured the siege of Jerusalem. Food had been a rare commodity as the Romans tried to weaken them before the final battle, but Thanoon had eaten well up until the start of this torturous journey.

The procession walked up the final incline and as they reached the summit, they could see the Roman jewel on the Mediterranean. Caesarea was spread out beneath them on the shores of a calm blue sea. In the distance, waves crested in front of golden sandy beaches. In front of the beach, stood the Amphitheater.

Thanoon gazed below but all he could concentrate on were two huge, white-marble statues on the side of the Roman road with large carvings of two heads prominently displayed on the top.

He looked at the statues and turned to one of the prisoners. "Who are they?" he asked as he nodded at the statues.

"Herod the Great and Herod Antipas, his son. Herod the great built Caesarea."

"May God damn them to hell!" Thanoon replied.

The prisoner nodded, pointing toward the sea at the Amphitheater. "That's where we're going. The only question is whether we are going to fight Gladiators, be mauled by animals or get mutilated in the Chariot races."

Thanoon was totally shocked at how a culture that could build things of such beauty as he saw below him could also be the purveyors of such cruelty. It was beyond his understanding.

All he could think of to say was, "These Romans are certainly barbaric. And they think we are uncivilized because we don't worship Caesar!"

Thanoon looked at his chain mate. "I at least hope we get quartered in the same school. I hear the Gladiator school feeds us well, so we will put up a good fight."

DEL LEADS THE WAY

HILAL'S QUMRAN CAVE - THE SAME DAY

Waking up in the quiet and darkness of a cave is a spooky experience. For a desert dweller used to waking up to a spectacular sunrise or, if early enough, to the retreat of the night stars back into obscurity, the black-as-coal nothingness of a completely dark cave was unsettling. Jude had just awakened to experience this solitude for the first time.

As he was rousing and stretching, out of the corner of his eye, he saw a strange shadow enter his cave. He jumped back startled by this intrusion as the big apparition gave an ear-shattering grunt and fell to the floor. The noise woke Mary, as well, and she rushed in. "What is it now?" she called out in a frightened voice.

Jude was still not sure. He was creeping forward to identify the heavy breathing he could hear. He called out to Mary, "Get the fire going and bring a lamp!"

As the light from the lamp approached, Mary exclaimed, "It is Thanoon's camel, El Deloua!"

She quickly busied herself looking over the camel, gravitating to its hind quarters where she saw the blood-and-sand-soaked wound on her flank. Mary knelt down to look at El Deloua's face, rubbing her forehead.

"Go get some water for her to drink and bring me some water and rags to clean her up."

Jude left in a hurry. "That is Thanoon's camel. He must be in trouble; he would never leave El Deloua."

Mary started working on the injured hind quarter while Jude tried to give the camel water. After she drank, as if revived, she tried to rise. Mary put a gentle hand to her neck encouraging her to lay still.

"You must stay put, El Deloua. You gave us quite a fright. But where is Thanoon?" If you are here by yourself, Thanoon must have run into trouble.

"Jude," she turned to her human counterpart, "this is just a flesh wound. Take her back to the stables. As far as I can tell, she is just dehydrated; she needs gallons of water."

For the next two days, Hilal's Qumran cave was more like a nursery than anything else. El Deloua was gaining her strength back and Mary had sewn up the cut on her flank. She foraged on the supplies in the stabling area, but seemed anxious, as if she needed to be back on her way to find her master.

Hilal was recovering, too. Spiritually, he was good; he was eating and feeling stronger, but the wounds on his back would take longer to heal. The mixture Mary had put on his back began to ease the pain as it helped the scar tissue stay supple.

Hilal was also very anxious. He was up and, against Mary's wishes, he was making preparations to leave, packing food supplies.

"I don't understand why you need to risk yourself going after Thanoon," Jude said in a questioning tone.

"He is my uncle, and for that reason alone, I need to go and rescue him. But, more importantly, he has also hidden the first consignment of scrolls in a cave around here. I don't know where they are, and if I don't rescue him, they might never be found. If they are not found all of our struggles will have been for naught."

Jude decided to help Hilal with his preparations. "Then I must go with you, Hilal. I must keep you safe."

"Jude you have done so much already that I never expected this of you. You have more than made up for all the difficult times you put me through when we were growing up."

"Hilal, although I will always be ashamed of the way I treated you in Wadi Zuballa when we were growing up, what I am now doing is not to make up for my bullying," Jude said thoughtfully. "You told me that you have forgiven me; I just hope that God does, too.

"I am doing this because, for the first time in my life, I have a purpose. You have given me so much more than I could have dreamed when I came to ask your forgiveness. You have given me a reason to live, a reason to hope."

Hilal was very surprised to hear Jude explain his feelings that way. "In that case, let's tighten the cinches around El Deloua and your camel, and we can be on our way, but I must tell you that it will be a very dangerous mission."

They were both quiet, content in their own thoughts as they finished their work. Hilal was nuzzling El Deloua. As he stood to her one side, stroking her neck, he whispered to her gently, "I sure hope you can help me find Thanoon. Jerusalem is a big place. In all the confusion, it is going to be a difficult task."

Jude heard Hilal speak to the camel, and he nodded his head in sympathy. Mary watched her two friends. She thought them both crazy and tried once more to dissuade them from taking this trip.

"Hilal," she said, "you are not strong enough to go on this rescue mission; you need more rest."

He looked over at his dear friend. "Mary, for almost 30 years, my uncle has been looking after me. This time, he needs me. If I don't go now, I might be too late to help him.

"A few more days delay may be more time than he has, and I have to find out what has happened to him. We should be back in a week. Wish us good fortune."

Mary gave them a wave and turned to walk away, the emotion of it all too much for her.

OUTSKIRTS OF JERUSALEM - THE NEXT DAY

The ride from Qumran to Jerusalem was an arduous one. It was only 25 miles as the crow flies, but across the desert, one can rarely travel as the crow flies. Obstacles had to be ridden around, soft sand that would swallow a man to his flanks with every step had to be avoided.

In the Negev, the ground was frequently below sea level, which meant the temperature extremes were intense. Leaving the fresh wind of the Qumran mountain area, one sank into the oppression and stillness of a type of hell. Everything was a shimmering mirage.

Jude would have been frightened by himself, but with Hilal leading the way, he was comforted.

Hilal and Jude approached the outskirts of Jerusalem. Not much had changed in the few days they had been away. Fires still smoldered and rotting carcasses were everywhere. Roman soldiers, still under Caesar's direct orders, were dismantling Jerusalem, tearing stone from stone.

Hilal tried to steer El Deloua toward Jerusalem to begin their search for Thanoon. As much as he tried, El Deloua resisted him. He kept turning El Deloua to the city, and she just kept insisting they go the other way, turning toward Caesarea.

The more Hilal cajoled her in his direction, the more she kept turning back to go in the other. In frustration, he decided to let her have her way on the off chance she knew what she was doing. He said out loud to Thanoon's camel, "I sure hope you know what you're doing, Del. We must find Thanoon soon."

As if she understood every word, El Deloua turned her big neck to look at Hilal and gave an almighty bellow.

"Alright, alright, we will go your way," he said.

Hilal and Jude continued along the road to Caesarea as Roman Legions marched along the road going in both directions. At nightfall, Hilal tried to pull El Deloua over to make camp, but she would not stop. Trying to encourage her, he leaned over to talk in her ear, "Del, you must stop to rest."

He tried to pull her up, but El Deloua just grunted and kept going. The moon came up, and still she plodded on. Many hours later, she finally stopped. Hilal and Jude were worn out by the long ride. By the time they stopped, it was too dark to see, so they just released their camels' cinches and settled down to rest.

The smell of putrefying flesh was overwhelming, and Jude, stretching and rubbing his back, said to Hilal, "I never knew riding a camel could be so painful, and the smell around here is terrible."

They sat down, placed a bedroll next to their camels and tried to sleep for the short time until dawn.

SEEKING THANOON

Hilal was the first to wake. El Deloua was already foraging close by. He looked over at her and realized in wonder that she was in no hurry this morning. As he stretched his back, he looked at his surroundings. Behind their camp was an aqueduct. He said to himself, "Well, I'll be, El Deloua. You bring us to an aqueduct in the middle of the desert."

Hilal gathered his empty water skins, went over to the support columns of the aqueduct and started to climb up. As he reached the top, Jude ambled over to watch him, but he was too busy filling his skins to pay much attention.

When he finished, Hilal watched some vultures pecking at carrion a little distance up the road. Curious, he climbed down the column, gave the water skins to Jude and told him, "I'll be back in a moment."

Jude thought nothing of it. It was common practice for people to seek a little privacy first thing in the morning. He walked back to their camp to start a fire, and Hilal walked over to see what the birds were eating.

As he got closer, the vultures objected to his presence, dancing around nervously, squawking as they went, but he saw they were feasting on human remains. Shocked by the unexpected site, he tried to restrain some dry heaves when he noticed that all the bodies had had their hands and feet neatly severed. Not able to find a logical reason for why this would be, he shook his head in a questioning manner and returned to water El Deloua.

When they had finished watering their camels, a party riding donkeys came by and stopped. The man leading the newcomers was older and not very healthy. He paused close to Hilal and Jude. Travelers meeting on the road in these times were very careful since violence, betrayal and theft were common occurrences.

The old man approached Hilal and asked him, "Could you spare any water for me and my family?

Hilal was alert, suspicious, but he wanted to help. Still, giving away his water could be a death sentence for his group. "We can't spare any water, but I will be happy to take your water skins up to the aqueduct and fill them for you."

The old man, surprised at his generosity responded, "That would be excellent. While you do that, I will brew some tea on your fire."

Hilal collected the stranger's skins and went back to the aqueduct to fill them. As his view was panoramic, he took a moment to look over the horizon to see if any danger approached. There was none, so he relaxed a little and descended the column to enjoy some morning tea.

On returning, the stranger and Jude were seated around a small fire brewing the tea. The stranger saw Hilal approaching. "Come join us. That is a beautiful camel you have over there."

Hilal, in a better mood now that he knew no danger approached, said, "Yes, she belongs to my uncle. I am searching for him. If this does not seem too indelicate, from the aqueduct, I noticed vultures feeding on some dead bodies over by the road. All the bodies have had their hands and feet neatly severed off."

Hilal paused then asked. "Do you know why?"

The stranger's mood changed, and all of a sudden he looked uncomfortable. He checked around the camp, as if to verify that no one could overhear what he was about to say "The Romans," he whispered in a conspiratorial tone.

Hilal did not understand. "The Romans? What do you mean?"

The stranger was clearly agitated. He paused some more before answering nervously. "When the Romans finished destroying Jerusalem, they picked up as many survivors as they could and chained them all together to force-march them to the Amphitheater in Caesarea for the games."

Hilal repeated the man's words, still unclear of the meaning. "For the games? What does that have to do with those bodies?"

The stranger must have thought Hilal dense. He now tried to be very specific. "Those are the remains of the sick who couldn't keep up."

Hilal's face showed he still did not understand. So the stranger explained, "When the sick fell, rather than take the time to unshackle them from the others, the Romans would hack off their hands and feet with their swords. 'Practice', they called it."

Hilal couldn't believe what he heard. The brutality of these invaders amazed him. Shaking his head in shock, he said, "That's terrible. How can an entire people be so inhumane, so brutal? It is unbelievable."

"If your uncle is missing, and he was strong enough to make the march, then odds are that he will be at one of the training schools at the Amphitheater in Caesarea."

ROMAN ROAD TO CAESAREA

Hilal and Jude didn't waste any time after learning this knew information. Bidding their new acquaintance good day, they took off again for Caesarea. They urged their mounts on as much as they could, feeling the urgency of Thanoon's plight. The first indication that they were getting close to Caesarea was the fresh sea smell brought in by the wind. Gone was the smell of putrefying bodies. In the sky, no vultures could be seen. Finally in the mid-afternoon, as they reached the crest of a hill, they saw down into the town and the beautiful blue Mediterranean shone in the distance.

Caesarea was a jewel tucked into an inlet on the coast with a semi-tropical climate, a much sought-after location that many of the political elite of the day chose for their residence.

Hilal and Jude approached the same white-marble statues Thanoon had walked past some days earlier. Even from the outskirts of town, the Amphitheater in the distance was clearly visible.

Hilal had been thinking and voiced his conclusion out loud, "Jude, I'm beginning to understand why my Uncle Thanoon likes El Deloua so much. She is one smart camel. If it wasn't for her insistence, we would still be looking for Thanoon in Jerusalem. I think we need to find someone to educate us about this Amphitheater."

Jude thought he finally might be able to make a contribution. He said to Hilal, "I don't think you know, Hilal, but before I came to seek your forgiveness in Jerusalem, I spent many years in Caesarea working for an old rabbi in the synagogue close to the Coliseum.

"It was he, in fact, that helped me understand that I needed to seek your forgiveness. His synagogue is close to the Amphitheater. We can talk to him, and he has a stable there."

SYNAGOGUE IN CAESAREA

Jude led Hilal through the streets of Caesarea to the old synagogue in the shadows of the temple in Caesarea.

After introductions, Hilal, Jude and the local rabbi sat on a bench inside the synagogue. Hilal was overcome with grief for his uncle and wasted no time in getting to the crux of the matter. "Rabbi, what can you tell me about the Amphitheater? I fear a friend of mine may have been taken there."

The rabbi had just seen the contingent of near-death prisoners marched through the streets of Caesarea. "Was he part of the prisoners that just arrived from Jerusalem?" he asked.

Hilal was still anxious because he only suspected his uncle was there. "I think so, Rabbi, but I don't know for sure. How do I find out?"

"It will be difficult to see your friend; the arena is comprised of a wooden floor covered by sand. That covers an elaborate underground structure, and that structure consists of a two-level, subterranean network of tunnels and cages beneath the arena where gladiators and animals are held."

Hilal was crestfallen. "Sounds like it will be impossible to find him."

The rabbi shook his head from side to side. "Not necessarily so. The arena is connected by underground tunnels to a number of points outside the Coliseum.

"Animals and performers are brought through the tunnels from nearby stables and barracks," he said. "The first thing to do is to find out to which barracks he has been taken. Each barracks has a schedule assigning when they go outside to train, and that will be your chance – your only chance.

"Soon, there will be a spectacular celebration to commemorate the victory in Jerusalem," the old rabbi said thoughtfully, adding ominously, "They are unlikely to survive that day."

FIND MY GOLD!

TITUS' PRIVATE QUARTERS

General Titus had a career-ending problem. Although he had wiped out nearly all visible Jewish resistance in Jerusalem, he had none of the Temple treasures. Without those treasures, his plan to become the next Caesar and return to Rome triumphantly at the head of a procession to celebrate his victory would prove an unfulfilled dream.

He paced up and down inside his tent alone. His staff knew his moods and left him alone, afraid to enter his domain for any reason. Anxiety written all over his face, he flexed his hands as he paced, thinking, angry, muttering to himself, "If I find the sneaky Christians that tricked me, I will personally pull them limb from limb."

He continued pacing until an idea came to mind and an expression of relief came over his face. "I must find my gold," he said aloud to the empty room. "It must be in Jerusalem; someone must know where it is."

He walked over to the tent entrance and pulled aside the flap to shout out, "Octavius! Get here NOW! I need you in my tent."

A few minutes later, an agitated Octavius sped into Titus' tent. He stood at attention and beat his sword against his shield to announce his presence then awaited the pleasure of his commanding officer. When Titus acknowledged his presence, he said, "General, Sir."

Titus was looking for any angles that might provide an answer to his dilemma. "Octavius, have you found any neighbors of the Rabbi Hilal that can tell us about the treasure?"

"One neighbor we can't find, but another says that Hilal had a Bedouin uncle that visited often. He thinks he saw the same uncle being taken by the Fifth Legion to the games in Caesarea. If he survived the trip, he is there, Sir."

"Don't the games start tomorrow with the opening ceremony?"

"Yes, Sir, it is the local celebration of our military victory over the Jews."

Titus chose to ignore the last comment. He was glad it was over, but it was not the type of campaign that made a military general proud, he thought.

He sat down, pondering his situation then looked up at his captain; the decision had been made. He felt he needed to be sure Octavius understood the severity of the situation.

General Titus, hissing like a venomous snake, said threateningly, "Captain, if you value your life, you are going to do exactly what I say. Get the strongest ten men in your legion; you are then going to march, double-time, to the training barracks in Caesarea. You should be there in time for the opening ceremony.

"You will find this man and bring him back to me, unharmed," Titus said, inches from Octavius now, emphasizing the last word. "You had better pray that he survived the trip."

Titus waited for this threat to sink in then he added. "Do I make myself clear, Captain?"

Octavius was not an ignorant man; he understood exactly what his general meant. If this man was dead, he would be, too.

"Yes, Sir!" he answered back sharply.

General Titus asked one last question, "What is this slave's name, Octavius?"

"I believe it is Thanoon, General."

Titus thought it wise to add some incentive for a positive outcome. "Captain, my spies inform me that the Temple held much more gold than we discovered. Rumor has it that there was even a second Menorah.

"Spread the word among our soldiers," Titus said, sidling up behind Octavius now, "the soldier who brings me those who hid our gold or know who did will have his hands filled with gold, as much as he can carry."

Octavius' eyes bulged with greed and excitement. "Yes, General. As you command."

He left General Titus' quarters in a total panic, walked over to his command post and began deciding who he should choose and how they could get to Caesarea on time. He summoned his officers on the way to the adjutant's command post; there was no time to lose.

TOO PROUD TO STAND

OVERLOOKING GLADIATOR TRAINING FIELD

Hilal narrowed down to two possibilities the lookout points he needed to watch from to see if he could find where Thanoon was training. Luckily for him, all of the training areas were close to the arena, one on the west side and one on the south.

At daybreak, he was in position to watch the training field. He waited patiently and after an hour on the south position, he moved to the west side. As there was no activity there, he decided to go back to his original lookout station.

Around mid-morning, his patience was rewarded, as his attention was diverted to the field in front of the barracks. A huge gladiator, Colossus, walked out of a tunnel leading a pack of trainees equipped with wooden swords and wooden shields.

They were a skinny bunch of misfits, dirty, fearful and unkempt with shaggy beards. They were the most unlikely looking people you could imagine to compete against gladiators – all except one, who didn't kowtow to the trainers, but stood tall and proud.

Hilal knew immediately it was his strong, defiant Uncle Thanoon. The gladiator trainers, equipped with metal swords, shields and helmets were a well-fed group of professional, fit, well-muscled assassins.

One trainee caught the attention of Colossus. He walked up to the man, pulled the poor soul by his hair, and threw him to the ground. Colossus shouted for all to hear, "I saw this Christian dog, kneeling, saying prayers to his God this morning! I want you all to beat him to..."

He was cut off in mid-sentence by Thanoon, who shouted even louder, "I am not a Christian. I am a Bedouin who is proud to believe in the Almighty God that is not of this world!" He added in an even louder voice, "Not some monkey in Rome!"

Colossus was a huge, hairy, muscled beast of a man; he must have had the strength of two regular gladiators. After hearing Thanoon's blasphemy, he drew himself up to the size of three men and stretched even taller in his anger as he moved toward the offensive Bedouin dog. He lunged at Thanoon, launching a sideways kick that knocked him in the gut and sent him flying through the air.

Hilal was mortified when he heard his uncle's rant – proud, rebellious and stupid. He said to himself, "Oh, Uncle, do shut up, or they will kill you."

Colossus was not done. He stood over the prone Thanoon, who was still trying to get his breath back. "You dare call our Caesar a monkey?"

Thanoon heard Colossus, and although he was hardly able to move, he started to rise. He turned his head to look at the behemoth of a man and smiled insolently. Colossus saw that arrogant look on the slave's face and that was enough to launch him into another fit.

Then Thanoon spat out, "And a truly ugly one he is, too! Not even a monkey would want to be related to that heathen."

Colossus had never been so angry or provoked before; he totally lost control as Thanoon's image was burnt into his subconscious. He would never forget this slave. He raised his sword, widened the arc even more with which he would strike then turned the flat surface toward Thanoon and released all that energy and hatred in one motion.

The force of the blow was so great that it again launched Thanoon up in the air before he fell back to the ground in blessed unconsciousness. Hilal watched in horror, praying for his uncle, hoping that he would stay in that unconscious state and keep his mouth closed.

Colossus had to forcefully make himself pull his eyes away from Thanoon as the gladiators under his command watched in awe, terrified that he might turn his anger on them next. Pointing to Thanoon, he ordered his men, "I want this one saved for the lions; do not kill him. Call me when he regains consciousness."

Hilal was overcome with fear and love for his uncle; he wiped some tears from his eyes as he gazed upon the unconscious man. As there was nothing he could do, he hurried back to the synagogue trying to think on the bright side that he had at least found Thanoon. As he walked back, he was torn between his love for his uncle and desire to save a loved family member and his divine destiny. If he failed and got himself killed rescuing Thanoon, that mysterious stranger from the Temple would be very upset indeed. What a mess, he thought. Thanoon had hidden more than half the scrolls in some place in Qumran, and he wouldn't be able to find them without Thanoon showing him the way.

CAESAREA SYNAGOGUE

Caesarea was designed by Herod with typical Roman efficiency and consequently there were none of the restricted alleyways of Jerusalem. Instead, the streets were efficient and straight. In short order, Hilal was back at the synagogue, where the rabbi and Jude were together reciting prayers.

They looked up as Hilal entered, still hyper and overcome with grief for his uncle.

He immediately launched into what he had found. "They are going to give Thanoon to the lions! What can we do?"

Jude was the first to answer, as if not understanding what Hilal meant. "The lions?"

The rabbi was calmer than Jude or Hilal. He explained, "The Romans are masters of showmanship. Lions are part of the opening ceremony. When unsuspecting slaves are released into the arena, the crowd goes wild with excitement and lions are then released for the entertainment of the crowd. It is actually quite barbaric to see the lions feast on slaves."

"I can't let that happen!" Hilal cried in a panic." What can we do?"

The rabbi was quite glum; he thought it a foregone conclusion. "There is nothing we can do."

Jude had a completely different countenance; he was quite animated all of a sudden. "Yes, there is..." he muttered thoughtfully in a low confidential whisper.

Hilal and the rabbi were totally surprised by this sudden change in Jude. It was as if he had taken charge. Finally, Jude had found an area where he knew more than Hilal, and he could help.

"Hilal, go to the arena tomorrow with a rope and hitch our camels close by for our escape."

This was more than Hilal could have dreamed – a ray of hope. But he was curious and wanted to know details. "What are you going to do?"

"Just be there tomorrow, and be ready."

Hilal was still not convinced. "Jude, you are crazy! What is the plan?"

Jude answered, getting up and gathering his few things, "I don't have time to tell you. Besides you'd never believe me if I did."

Jude left to the total astonishment of Hilal and the rabbi.

INTO THE ARENA

THE ROMAN AMPHITHEATER

There were crowds and crowds of people swarming the outside of the Amphitheater the next morning. Word had spread that this was going to be a spectacular celebration and the level of excitement in the crowd was evidenced by the very loud buzz of conversation and laughter, everyone waiting for the gates to be opened, so they could get the best seats.

This was a family event, most came with their children and everyone dressed in their finery, colorful clothes and fancy hairstyles, as if they had been preparing for this outing for a week or more.

The Port of Caesarea was by now the biggest in the world with ships from all around the Roman Territory arriving and bringing the very best the world had to offer from all points. Perfumes, the finest silks, the best wines, whatever the empire had to offer could be bought at the markets of Caesarea.

In anticipation of the gates opening, the music started. Crowds pushed against the entrance gates, the excitement now electric, orchestrated by festival organizers who used the music and fanfare to hype up the crowd. Thunderous applause could already be heard by the political elite that had already entered the stadium.

After everyone had entered, it was time. Inside the arena, clowns had been running around, enticing the crowd to laughter by their funny antics. But now they left, the music slowly decreased in volume. As the level of music in the arena went down, the level of expectation went up. The atmosphere was charged and tense. Everyone sat down and the sudden silence was infectious.

In the total silence, everyone sat mesmerized, waiting for the next act. In the arena, a reinforced gate opened noisily, and the crowd strained to see what was happening. Three slaves were pushed out into the arena. They were confused, not knowing what to expect. They lifted their arms to their foreheads, straining to see in the sudden bright light. They looked around at the crowd, mystified, seeing no gladiators. In confusion, they walked around aimlessly not knowing what was happening.

Across the arena from the confused slaves, Hilal was seated at the lowest level, near an exit, Jude, 180 degrees opposite. They had been searching the crowd for each other, when their eyes locked and they nodded in acknowledgement of one another, both praying for good fortune. Hilal was also praying that Jude knew just what he was doing.

Down in the arena, the slaves were still looking around and stumbling aimlessly about the arena as the music started again and the crowd began to cheer.

The music and drums reached a crescendo. Suddenly the crowd and the music fell silent, and noisy chains could be heard, clanging together, the sound ominous. A loud screeching sound followed, the sound of tortured lumber being pulled against its will. Slowly, three doors to the underground chambers opened up from the floor of the arena. No one could see what was rising from underneath; it was too dark. The crowd remained silent in anticipation; the slaves stood confused, looking to the doors.

Out of the darkness, the outline of something appeared and began to take shape. Large, hairy heads peered from the black hole and on either side of the face two shining, golden-colored eyes seem to glow.

People in the crowd were sitting on the edge of their seats, staring to see, struggling to recognize the beasts. Suddenly, one lion charged from his door, stopped and waited for his eyes to adjust to the blinding light. The crowd was shocked by the brazen entrance of a gigantic male lion. They sat back in panic, as if trying to get away from the danger. Down in the arena, the three slaves also saw the lion appear.

After this much time with no apparent danger, the slaves had begun to think – no to hope – that they might survive this day, that their fears had been a big misunderstanding. Then the first lion appeared, and their hope vanished.

Two slaves stood still, too shocked to move. Thanoon was the third slave. He fell to his knees, head bowed and hands raised together, praying. The crowd suddenly started another round of loud applause; another lion had leapt up out of his door and stopped, then a third.

The crowd became very quiet then, almost in pity for the slaves. The men looked around, comprehension spreading on their faces, then fear, and finally, the certainty of what was going to happen.

The lions moved toward their intended victims. They acted ravenous, licking their chops; they had been purposefully kept without food for a week. From one end of the crowded stalls, a lone figure jumped into the arena, carrying two large bags. The crowd's attention turned. He had snapped the tension, and they erupted in applause again, thinking this was part of the show. He ran toward the lions and, with a massive effort, threw his two bags in the center of the beasts. Giant sewer rats freed from their captivity ran out of the bags in all directions, hundreds of them. The lions were confused. They stopped and looked all around them. One lion ran away from the rats, another chased them, and the third simply stood still. The rats were also scared, fleeing for their lives.

The lone figure did not stop. He went straight toward Thanoon grabbed his arm, and shouted to him, "Run! Run like your life depends on it!"

Thanoon started to move, still in shock. As he began to run, from the crowd came a giant yell of rage as Colossus realized this was not part of the show. He stood up, pushed spectators to the floor, and rushed to the arena wall. He jumped into the arena, running, yelling at Thanoon.

Thanoon looked at Colossus running toward him, pulling his sword from his scabbard. He began to run, but Colossus was too fast. He caught up to Thanoon, and, with one almighty fist, he slapped the weakened slave to the ground. Colossus stood in front of Thanoon and raised his sword to decapitate him.

Behind Colossus, one lion recovered his wits and roared with hunger and anger. He eyed the confusion in the ring then his eyes settled on the biggest meal, Colossus. The lion charged just as Colossus had his sword raised to its maximum height. Colossus did not see the beast, nor did he perceive that the crowd had become quiet, until he heard a roar from behind him.

Colossus saw Thanoon turn looking at something else instead of his executioner. He turned to look, as well, just in time to see the lion's mouth wide, head high, as it barreled toward him. The beast knocked him to the floor. Just then, the other two lions recovered their wits and ran over to join the massacre, tearing Colossus to pieces.

Jude turned to Thanoon. "Weren't you praying for a miracle?" Without waiting for an answer, he shouted, "RUN!"

They both ran as fast as they could toward Hilal who dangled a rope over the side of the arena wall. Thanoon didn't need help; he was over the top with lightning speed. Hilal extended a hand to Jude and hauled him over.

The crowd roared its approval, still thinking this was part of the entertainment. The spectators parted to make way for Thanoon and Jude as they ran for the exit. The crowd was still applauding loudly, enjoying the unexpected twist.

Hilal watched their rear, ready for any challenge, but there was no resistance, no guards. It was all so unexpected that no one suspected this was a real escape. As they exited the arena, El Deloua saw her master running like the devil toward her and announced her approval by grunting loudly. Hilal followed them out surprised by the ease with which they were able to escape.

They all mounted their camels and sped away.

THE ARENA - MOMENTS LATER

Octavius led his troop of 10 Roman Soldiers, two abreast, stoically marching at double-time, toward the arena. They had marched for twelve hours straight and badly need a rest, the weight of their armor and weapons adding at least fifty pounds to their load.

As they arrived, they found the slave master leaving the arena furious. In the background, sounds of all types of cheering and jeering came from the arena.

The Roman captain saluted the slave master and shouted loudly over the noise, "Hail, Caesar!"

The slave master replied matching his volume, "Hail, Caesar!"

Octavius was having a hard time regulating his breathing because he was so tired. "On orders of General Titus," he paused to catch his breath, "we are looking for one of your slaves. Do you have the slave, Thanoon, here?"

The slave master's response was to gawk at Octavius, speechless. Octavius repeated his orders. "Bring him here. We are to take him to General Titus in Jerusalem."

The slave master finally found his tongue, "Well, Captain…" he began. "Your prisoner was here this morning. He was part of the opening ceremony…to feed the lions."

Hearing these words, the Roman captain of the troop looked at the slave master with incredulity, dread spreading on his face.

"He escaped."

Octavius was flabbergasted, but secretly relieved. "Escaped, you say? How?"

"You wouldn't believe me if I told you. But he is getting away. He took the road to Jerusalem, not five minutes ago."

Octavius turned to his men, "Troop, about turn! Double-time! Back to Jerusalem!"

Since he had already turned to face the way back to Jerusalem, he was not able to see the murderous looks he got from his men. If they weren't so tired, mutiny was in their eyes.

TITUS'S PRIVATE QUARTERS - JERUSALEM

The chosen ten – Octavius' strongest runners – arrived back on Mount of Olives at General Titus' camp in the early evening of the next day, exhausted. There was only one reason for the fast pace of the return – to inform Titus of Thanoon's escape. Octavius feared for his life – much less his career – if there were any delay in the relay of this information.

Upon arriving back in Jerusalem, Octavius went straight to General Titus' private quartets. His leader did not beat around the bush. "What news, Captain? Do you have my slave?"

Octavius answered with the most positive thing he could think of to say, "No, Sir, but he is alive. He escaped from the coliseum before we got there."

General Titus looked at Octavius long and hard. Octavius was getting more anxious with every second.

"What is your name, Captain?"

"Octavius, General."

"Were you the eighth child?"

"Eighth son, General."

Titus had been making small talk while he made his decision. "I am in need of a new adjutant here in Judea."

Octavius bowed slightly at Titus, it looked like it was in respect for his commanding officer but was, in fact, a reflex action as if he was about to throw up, such was his nervousness.

General Titus didn't notice, he continued his thought process. "Our Roman legions have finished their work here; the rebellion is squashed. I am going to return to Rome with our treasures," he said. "Thanoon must be found. I want you to take as many men into the desert as you need, find him, find out where my gold is hidden.

"When you find my gold, you will be a rich man and my new adjutant," Titus said, smiling "How does Adjutant to Caesar Titus feel, Captain?"

Octavius was overwhelmed. "Very good, General," he said modestly.

"Find my slave, and you will be Caesar's adjutant."

Octavius was dismissed. He needed to rest as well as let his most reliable ten rest. He had to have time to plan the next phase of the Thanoon campaign, as he decided to call it.

The next morning, he assembled his men. The previous night, before he had retired, he had sent 100 men out into Jerusalem to see if anyone could learn any information on the whereabouts of Thanoon.

Octavius assembled his officers. "What news of our search, men? Do we have any fresh leads?"

All of his men shook their heads side to side, their faces reflecting their frustration. "No one will talk to us, Captain."

Octavius was slightly surprised by this, and asked them, "Why?"

"Everyone knows that the goldsmiths were asked for help and when they volunteered, they were tricked and crucified, Sir."

The Roman captain reflected the sentiments of all the men who had spent the night searching. "That imbecile, Flavius, crucified all of our informants. No wonder General Titus executed him."

Then he added, "We will celebrate tonight, but tomorrow we must start again with renewed vigor or the General may be coming after us if we fail."

He watched his men to see if this had the desired effect. It did, so he continued, "Tomorrow, we leave for the desert. We will search the sands until we find him."

One of his men said, "That's a very big desert out there. How do we know where to look?"

Octavius had spent most of last night pondering this same question. He answered, "Before Hilal was captured, he led us to the south, obviously a false trail. To the west is the sea and much too populated. From Caesarea in the north, Thanoon ran east with his accomplices. To the east we go to the mountains around the Dead Sea. That is where we will start our search, the mountains of the Dead Sea."

SURROUNDED

QUMRAN CAVES IN THE DEAD SEA MOUNTAINS

The return trip for Hilal, Thanoon and Jude from Caesarea was an arduous one. They did not dare take the well-travelled Roman road to Jerusalem. Word of their escapade had undoubtedly spread. Thanoon's condition would also cause alarm.

Although he had managed to run out of the arena in Caesarea, once the adrenalin rush of that experience wore off, he was in a greatly weakened state, hardly able to ride by himself. They took off across the desert but after many miles, Thanoon was too frail to ride and the camel that Jude was riding went lame. Hilal couldn't slow down and he could not afford to share a camel with Jude. With much emotion, they parted company. Jude would head back to Wadi Zuballa, and Hilal and Thanoon would continue on to Qumran.

After Jude left, the last day's ride was down beneath sea level, the hottest, most humid, sticky stretch of mirage-prone hell Hilal had ever witnessed. It was fortunate that Thanoon was close to unconsciousness and strapped to El Deloua. They plodded on through the worst of the day. As hot afternoon was about to turn into a sticky dusk, Hilal thought he smelled the first signs of getting close to the Dead Sea.

Slowly their route seemed to rise out of the depths of the humid plain toward the now visible mountains. Hilal found the wadi he was looking for and, after a quick check to see if anyone followed them, he travelled down into the riverbed to follow the ancient trail to their cave. He was dog tired, travel weary and dusty.

Thanoon, in his oblivion and tied to his El Deloua, was too sick to ride. As they approached the thorn-bush hidden entrance, Hilal sat tall, glad to be close to home. He dismounted and led El Deloua and his camel into the cave.

By now, Mary had heard their approach and came running out of hiding exclaiming, "Who is that?

"It is Thanoon; he is in bad shape."

Hilal and Mary carried Thanoon inside the cave to the area where Mary had been sleeping. She helped Hilal lay him down gently, and with a great tenderness that Hilal had not noticed before, she started cleaning his wounds.

Thanoon felt the tender, caressing touch and opened his eyes in pleasure, looked at Mary and squeezed her hand. He smiled before drifting back to sleep. Mary enjoyed his reaction, as if some special bond had been affirmed between them. She smiled a deep, caring smile, a look that only a woman in love could give.

A little later, Mary came out to see Hilal.

"I think he is going to be alright," she said. "But it seems he has two broken ribs. I have bound them as well as I can. It will be a long recovery. What happened to him?"

"You know Thanoon; he picked a fight with a monster three times his size."

Hilal's face contorted at the painful memory of that conflict with Colossus. He continued, "But we got him back, and that monster is dead."

Then Hilal added, as if it was the furthest thought in his mind, "What of the scrolls? Did you get them out of Jerusalem safely? Are they here... safe?"

Nodding her head toward a storage area, Mary confirmed for him, "They are all there."

GENERAL TITUS' CAMP

At daybreak, Octavius stood before 100 Roman legions assembled in full battle dress. Many military generals throughout history have been known to be ego maniacs. To understand, one only has to stand in command of a gathering of 10,000 battle-ready, hardened warriors, willing to march forward to their deaths if ordered. Octavius found himself in such a situation as he addressed his troops.

"Soldiers, today, we march for Caesar; today, we finish our mission in Judea. Tonight, we camp in the mountains of the Dead Sea. Then we will find the last of the Christian traitors and find out what we need to know. Then we can go back to Rome...

"For now, MARCH, double-time! Tonight, we drink wine and rest at the Dead Sea."

HILAL'S QUMRAN CAVE

An ominous mood hung over the three friends as they woke in Hilal's cave. They were tense, the feeling of impending doom prevalent. Thanoon and Hilal sat together around a fire in the cave.

Hilal could not shake his feeling that they were facing an imminent calamity. He looked at his uncle and said, "We are in danger. I had a vision last night. The Romans are coming."

Thanoon was still moving slowly, recovering from his beating at the hands of Colossus. "You mean they are coming to the caves. But how? They don't know anything about this place."

Hilal was insistent. "I don't know how they know, but I am sure they are coming. We cannot let them get here, we must do something." Then, as if checking how much help Thanoon would be, he asked, "How are you feeling, Uncle?"

"Mary has a magical touch. I am feeling much better already. Another day or two, and I should be back to normal."

Hilal was unusually glum this morning. "Another day might be all we have."

Mary joined them. "Hilal," she said looking sternly at him, "Thanoon is not ready for any more of your crazy schemes. He needs time to recover."

Hilal winked at Thanoon, who was beaming like a bright fire. He tried to respond back cheerfully at them. "My crazy schemes, huh?"

Then he saw that they were not paying much attention to him, just holding hands and looking at each other. He felt like the odd man out, so he said, "I'll leave you two love birds to it then."

Later that night, Thanoon and Hilal left to climb to the highest point of the mountains. They cautiously made their way on a moonless night. As they approached the top, there was an ominous glow of light coming up from the peaks below. They looked down to the valley floor together and saw the light of hundreds of campfires of the Roman camp. They could picture below them hordes of soldiers drinking wine, celebrating noisily.

Hilal asked Thanoon in a whisper, "How many chariots do you count?"

"There must be at least 200. Each chariot has two men and two horses."

Hilal nodded in agreement. "The whole Roman army in Judea must be down there. I think we have seen enough, we are in serious trouble.

They settled back from the edge of the peak. "There must be 5,000 soldiers down in the valley," Hilal said. "I'm not sure if we can escape this one."

Thanoon had seen something that peaked his interest. "I think I saw that Roman captain, Octavius, down below. He is the vermin that arrested me, sent me to the coliseum." He added vehemently, "I pray to your God and on all I hold holy that I can personally sever his head from his body."

Hilal looked at his uncle in understanding. "Our God," he affirmed. "We need to get back to Mary."

When Hilal and Thanoon returned, Mary had coffee brewing. She could tell by their concerned faces that they did not bring good news.

Thanoon went over to Mary and clasped her hand. He looked her in the eyes and said to her, "The Romans are here, camped down in the valley. It doesn't look good." He touched her cheek as she looked down, defeated and afraid. "I will not let them get to you, Mary."

Mary smiled at Thanoon in total trust and affection.

Hilal tried to cheer everyone up saying, "Let us see what tomorrow brings. At dawn, we must be back on the summit to try to ferret out their plan.

MINOR MIRACLES AND HOPELESSNESS

THE DEAD SEA MOUNTAINS - THE NEXT MORNING

The next morning brought no better news. Before they even left the cave to climb up to their lookout point, they could hear the fanfare coming from the Roman camp. The commotion of an awaking army – loud voices shouting orders, horses neighing in rebellion to their harsh treatment as they were being harnessed to chariots.

As they started their climb, they smelled the charcoal of campfires, and a sense of foreboding accompanied the two friends on their way to the summit. Once there, they crawled on their bellies to peek down at the camp below as it assembled. Fires were being extinguished as slaves helped soldiers dress for battle. Horses were made ready.

Hilal counted chariots and, by his reckoning, they were right – 200. They stood ready in two columns, each column two-abreast. The excitement of the horses was evident by their frisky behavior. At least 5,000 foot soldiers stood ready with their platoons. Ominously, the Roman camp fell silent and all heads turned to their commanding officer.

Octavius was dressed in all his splendor, a bronze galea, a Roman soldier's helmet, on his head with a face mask decorated with a fish as a type of crest. He rode a black stallion, trotting majestically, pulling his head against the reins from left to right in excitement, as he proudly lifted his front knees to chest height. All eyes watched him prance to the front.

The Captain reined in his horse, turned it to face the assembled army, and sat, letting the tension mount. It seemed to every soldier that the commanding officer looked him individually in the eye.

When Octavius judged the moment to be opportune, he stood in his stirrups, his red cloak tied by a gold chain around his neck flapping in the wind. He lifted his sword and held it in line from his belly button to his nose. He shouted at the top of his voice, "HAIL, CAESAR!"

The assembled soldiers in front of Octavius shouted back at him, pummeling the hilt of their swords against their chest body armor in a thunderous monotone, "HAIL, CAESAR!"

Up above, on the mountain ridge, Hilal and Thanoon felt the vibration of that deafening roar. It shook the very ridge upon which they lay. The sound of the sword hilts hitting the body armor took on a single beat as they all began to respond in time to one another. Gradually, the metal clang gave way to a stamping of feet, pounding the sod in perfect harmony.

The deafening barrage astounded Hilal and Thanoon, the display of military might intimidating. Finally, the clamor died down, and Octavius, still standing in his stirrups, lifted his hands up as if a maestro orchestrating his symphony.

As he sat down, he lowered his hands. The assembled soldiers obeyed, imperceptibly at first, as those in the front rows slowly stopped hammering against their shields, then row by row the noise subsided, the stamping feet ceased, even the dust slowly started to obey and return to the ground.

Once all was quiet again, Octavius stood in his stirrups and bellowed to his adrenalin-filled assembly, "The men we are seeking have stolen General Titus' gold. Do not kill them! Anyone we find is to be brought to me for questioning.

"These slaves must be found!" he shouted. "We are going to form a line to the north of the mountain range, running east to west. In the valley, we will station our chariots, 100 to the east and 100 to the west. They will give chase in case anyone tries to flee."

He paused a moment before continuing. "Soldiers will maintain their line east to west as we go over every inch of these mountains. Every cave and hidden hole is to be explored," he emphasized. "The platoon that finds our thieves will be given as much gold as they can carry."

He stopped to let that sink in then rose again even higher on his stallion, shouting at the top of his lungs, "HOO----RAH!"

The soldiers echoed back at him equally loudly, "HOOORAH! HOOOORAH!"

The ground reverberated again with stamping feet and swords hitting shields. Octavius conducted his soldiers to silence again by lowering his arms. He spoke now in a lower tone, the soldiers almost breaking formation to lean forward trying to hear him. "They are here; we will keep searching until we find them. Move out."

On the ridge above, Thanoon and Hilal turned around and looked at each other. This was not good news. Silently they started back for their cave. The sadness in their eyes spoke for them of the finality of the coming invasion of Roman soldiers. So awesome in its power, they were speechless.

After crawling down from the summit, they waited to stand until they could do so without being seen. They rose, still speechless, overcome with grief. They did not need to verbalize their thoughts; they knew they were together until the end.

Their somber mood and feeling of impending doom did not abate as they re-entered their Qumran hideout. Mary was there to greet them and had not expected good news. Her intuition was confirmed by the looks on their faces.

The friends assembled around the fire to enjoy the brew Mary had prepared. Without preamble Hilal announced defiantly, "Today we will stay here. I hope they do not discover us on the first pass. These Romans want only the gold, they don't know about the scrolls. If we survive today, I will let myself be captured tomorrow and lead them back to Jerusalem."

Thanoon did not look up from his steadfast stare at the fire as he responded, "I cannot let you do that, Hilal. I will go. Besides, they think you are dead. You have work to do here."

Mary looked at her two companions as if they had lost their minds. Totally rejecting both of their ideas, she said, "Thanoon you cannot do that. If you go, we all go together."

The three friends now looked from one to another, none willing to see another sacrificed to the Romans.

Thanoon was the first to break the silence. "No, it is I who must go."

Hilal saw that this was going nowhere, so he decided to change track. "I will keep watch over the front of the cave; hopefully our thorn bush will keep us hidden."

The morning passed with the tension mounting inside the cave. The view from the entrance was very restricted, and they could only hear the unusual clatter of small rocks being dislodged by passing feet and the occasional words being spoken. It was clear that Roman soldiers were getting closer as the search progressed, getting louder. They approached the wadi that led to the entrance.

Hilal was at his wit's end, the tension of the unknown, unbearable. He could stand it no longer and stealthily crept up to the entrance to look out from the behind the thorn bush. He saw soldiers beating bushes coming toward them.

It looked like the end, he thought, as he tearfully watched their approach. Suddenly, his attention was diverted from the soldiers and up the hillside from the cave where the Roman searchers had scared some wildlife. He watched as the panicked herd of mountain goats scampered up the mountain away from the Romans. The soldiers' attention was immediately diverted away from the search to the possibility of roasted goat for dinner.

The small party of Romans was instantly thrown into pandemonium. Gone was the lined formation, searching by their coordinates. The hungry soldiers saw their dinner fleeing up the mountain.

One soldier was clearly more interested in the goats than his orders. "Get your spears, men! That's dinner! Fresh goat meat."

The soldiers ran after the goats, but the goats were far more agile climbers and reached a safe distance easily. They turned to watch their pursuers with infuriating indifference and curiosity, as if to question their sanity. Hilal maintained his watch and saw the soldiers frantically try to close the gap. One stopped, readied his spear, and, with an incredible thrust, launched it at the flock. The spear was the perfect parabolic curve of death, gliding through the air noiselessly. The goats stayed still, watching. They could not see the lightening rod of their demise coming toward them.

Their one mistake was being bunched all together. The spear finished its upward ascent and started its slow curve back to earth. The soldiers watched with exaggerated stillness; all was quiet, until the flock of goats, minus one, took off in a panic again. Hilal heard them shouting encouragement as they ran to see if the throw was successful.

The emotional toll this was taking on a Hilal was almost unbearable. Although the relief he felt from the near-divine appearance of the mountain goats was overwhelming, the hopelessness of their predicament was crushing. He made his way back into the interior of the cave. Thanoon and Mary watched him pass by, sensing that he needed some time to himself.

Thanoon had taken up the lookout position at the front of the cave. As darkness descended, he returned to find Mary busily making some food. Thanoon approached from the entrance as Hilal came back from his self-imposed solitude. He said to his uncle, "Thanoon, I cannot let you make this sacrifice."

Thanoon was equally adamant, "You must."

Turning to Mary, Thanoon pleaded with her with his eyes. "You must promise me that you will not do anything stupid."

Hilal realized, once again, that this conversation was going nowhere, so he said determinedly, "I will go with you in the morning to our lookout. In the meantime, I am going to pray."

He left Thanoon and Mary huddled together, looking at the fire in a trancelike posture.

RISE OF THE DEAD SEA

The next morning, Hilal came out to the living area to see Mary and Thanoon already dressed and waiting for him. Hilal knew his uncle wanted to be sure that he did not sneak off to do something rash. The three of them left the cave in the predawn darkness to return to their lookout.

The walk up to the peak was quiet, each immersed in his or her own thoughts. As they approached the top, the fires from the Roman camp below illuminated their position and they all started crawling on their bellies at the last moment, fearing that they would make a silhouette for the watching Romans.

Three sets of eyes looked over the ridge onto the camp as the rising sun began to light up the escarpment below, giving them a clearer view. The scene was almost identical to the day before. Slaves were busy over fires, making some type of cornmeal for breakfast while stable hands readied the horses.

Mary was the first to pick up on an unusual phenomena – the wind was changing directions. She looked to the south to see ominous black clouds forming. She nudged Thanoon. He looked at her and she nodded to the south. He followed her eyes to see the dark horizon just as Hilal noticed, as well. He shrugged his shoulders as if to say so what?

As the wind got stronger, soldiers down in the camp looked southward. Word soon spread, and more soldiers started to look southward. As they watched, a huge sand devil formed. Most of the preparations in the camp below stopped as everyone looked at this rising wonder. Most didn't know what to think as the twirling sand got ever stronger, coming toward the Roman camp. They stood motionless, not aware of any danger.

The horses were watching and they nervously started pulling against their halters, whinnying in fright. The stable hands tried to comfort them, stroking their necks or foreheads. The horses' panic became more widespread, and the Romans realized it was now a threat that they were watching.

An officer shouted, "Hold those horses still!"

The horses' fear spread to the men who began a nervous chatter among themselves. Suddenly, a huge light filled the sky and a single, gigantic bolt of lightning unleashed its fury down on the camp. It was a direct hit on a horse and his handler, and both evaporated in a cloud of steam, dust and smoke, leaving behind smoldering carcasses.

For a momentary span of time, every man and every animal, stood motionless, stunned by what they had just seen. Another solitary bolt of lightning sent its charge of electricity directly into the Dead Sea. The impact of this bolt was so strong it sent an ear-drum-wrenching explosion across the desert plain.

The horses reared up in total desperation and fear of the unknown. They were so frightened that their adrenalin-soaked muscles gave them enough strength to gallop away, dragging handlers with them that were unfortunate enough not to have let go. Soldiers unlucky enough to be in the way of the stampeding horses tried to flee for their lives. Others saw these soldiers running for their lives and started to run as well.

The Roman camp was in total panic. Even Octavius' black stallion was beyond control. He reared up, unseated the captain unceremoniously and charged after his fleeing kindred. Screams of alarm and fear rose from throughout the camp.

As the mist cleared from over the sea, a huge wall of water began to build. The barrage of water was so terrifyingly large that it grabbed the attention of the fleeing soldiers who stopped in their tracks, now totally awestruck. Another massive blast of air was unleashed on the camp, and many were blown off their feet as campfires were scattered, sending red hot embers into anything that would burn. All of the tents were set afire.

Soldiers now began to show real panic; not knowing the danger they faced, they ran in all directions, some knocking each other over. To add to the frenzy, a strange, high-pitched, piercing, whaling, evil sound of supernatural proportions started to envelope the camp. Soldiers looked at each other as if the very devil was chasing them.

Hilal, Mary and Thanoon watched. No wind even rustled their hair. They, too, were awestruck by the power of the devastation. Mary's eyes grew bigger by the moment as she cuddled closer to Thanoon. He protectively put his arm around her.

Panicked Roman soldiers were still trying to get away from the terror of the approaching wall of water rising out of the Dead Sea. It was so large that the crest seemed to disappear into the clouds. As the bank of water approached from the south, another ominous sound, like the screeching of the devil, came from the direction in which the soldiers were fleeing. A gut-wrenching tear of Biblical proportions seemed to be ripping earth and rock apart. A massive crevice started to form, cutting off their escape.

Those who thought they were lucky enough to be in the lead of the terrified swarm of soldiers leaving camp were the closest to the rapture of the earth. As quickly as they could, they tried to stop their advance. Behind them, their comrades were trying to catch up and couldn't see the giant abyss opening ahead. As the front runners tried to stop, the first round of laggards ran into them and pushed them into the ground or ran with them, careening into the gorge from hell opening in front of them.

The sound of earth and rock tearing apart was getting even louder. Not only were soldiers still fleeing the tidal wave from the south, but the ravine was tearing up more ground, getting closer and larger, and day was turning into night.

Out of the darkness on the Dead Sea side, the huge wall of water charged to the shore, every moment more ominous, it rose higher and higher until it seemed to reach the very heavens. As the water hit the sand, it seemed the top of the torrent kept moving faster while the lower part was slowing down over land. As the top of the wave had no support underneath it, gravity took over bringing the torrent crashing down in a crescendo of destruction over the deserted Roman camp.

Now that mass of water was struggling for space on the ground below, sweeping up all in its path until it reached the crevice that had cut off retreat to the north. The wall of water had cut off retreat to the south.

The terrified souls who had made it to the side away from the advancing water and the gorge were now besieged by mysterious ghost-like figures rising out of the ground around the ravine. They screamed ghoulish sounds as they flew out to pick a target among the stupefied soldiers who remained to the east and west. The mysterious creatures swooped down to grab a terrified victim with supernatural strength, lift him up and fly away while the victim pleaded for mercy, legs and arms kicking in abject terror.

As the ghouls reached the ravine, the slobbering, terrified victim was released in mid-flight to tumble into the steaming gorge. The survivors on the sides were terrified, screaming with fear. The ghostlike figures released one victim then returned to swoop down and choose another heathen soul, picking up soldiers and dropping them into the raging waters from hell.

The water made a final push from the south, rushing in and forcing all life in front of it toward the crevice, the ground behind it swept clean.

The piercing sounds from hades abated slowly, as every life form in the camp was wiped out and it seemed the ravenous appetites of the ghouls from the center of the earth were satiated. Soon there was no life below except for one man, who was unceremoniously thrown from his black stallion.

Octavius, alone, dressed in his uniform, clutching his shield and sword, ran in circles, confused and terrified. He ran from the crevice and the camp to the mountains of the Dead Sea.

THE LONDON CONNECTION

LIBRARY OF BOODLE'S CLUB – LONDON 1950S

"Good Heavens, George, did you see this news from Jerusalem?" asked Sebastian, one of two older members of London's elite aristocratic club known as Boodle's.

They sat in the large book-lined library reading their morning newspaper, attired in their evening dress. An equally formally dressed servant arrived with the tea service, and they stopped to enjoy a cup of the warm beverage before continuing with their silent reading.

George looked up from his newspaper, picked up his cup of tea and turned to his friend. "What?"

"Apparently, some young Bedouin shepherd boy might have unearthed one of the most significant Biblical finds of all times," Sebastian answered with excitement in his voice.

Sebastian began reading the story to his friend, *"In a long-untouched cave in the Qumran region on the shores of the Dead Sea, a Bedouin shepherd boy's search for a lost goat led to the discovery of eleven scroll-yielding caves, and evidence of ancient habitation..."*

George abruptly interrupted him. "Good Heavens, man. You don't actually believe that rubbish, do you?"

Sebastian looked up, frowning. "Why do you have to be so negative? I admit to a skeptic like you, it might seem doubtful, but Qumran was abandoned almost two thousand years ago during the time of the Roman incursion of 68 A.D."

"Why in Heaven's name would they hide these religious artifacts in the middle of the desert?"

Sebastian paused for a moment to enjoy the last sip of tea in his cup before continuing. "The Jews knew that the Romans wanted to destroy Jerusalem and burn any memory of their cultural and religious legacy. How else could they get the Jews to pay homage to Caesar? We know that anything of historical value that was left in Jerusalem was destroyed in the war of 70 A.D."

George fought back the urge to laugh at his friend and replied, "You are such a romantic, Sebastian. I bet you any amount of money those artifacts are fakes."

"The devil has an ally in a heathen like you, George! Do you want to put your money where your mouth is?"

George jumped at the opportunity. "Absolutely! But why the sudden confidence? Are you holding something back that will give you an edge in the bet?"

Sebastian put down his paper and looked directly at George. "I have just read that the reason the translation of the scrolls is slow to come out is because those fool French zealots at the Ecole Biblique are in charge of the dig and the scrolls."

"And just what is the Ecole Biblique?"

"My friend, you ought to know a little more about the subject before you throw your money away on bets with me," Sebastian said. "Ecole Biblique is a tool of the Roman Catholic Church and the Vatican, established in 1890 by the French LaGrange family. Their express intent is to hide and destroy relics that come to the surface that could harm the Roman Catholic Church."

"I don't believe that," George replied. "Besides, you know that I am half French."

"Well, I am going to finance an archaeology dig in Qumran," Sebastian said, with excitement in his voice. "Someone needs to keep the LaGrange people honest. If the scrolls are legit, you pay for half the cost of the expedition. Deal?"

Without hesitation, George answered, "Deal!"

CATCHING A BREAK

QUMRAN 1952

So far, Sebastian had had a very frustrating start to his archaeological expedition. The near-monopoly that the 'Ecole Biblique' had on the discovery was very frustrating. He sat in his tent, talking to Zayed, a shepherd boy who had been hired and fired by the Ecole Biblique. He was from the same tribe of Bedouins who lived in the vicinity of the cave.

Sebastian needed a break and he was willing to talk to anyone who could further his aim. "Why did the Ecole Biblique fire you?"

"I discovered the caves, so I wanted to be involved and learn about the scrolls," Zayed paused as if thinking bitterly about his treatment. "They told me that I was an ignorant Arab, and I should be grateful that I am not still tending my father's goats."

Sebastian was openly surprised that anyone would treat someone that way. "Quite arrogant, wouldn't you say?"

After all, if it weren't for this young boy, this whole tale of mystery and intrigue would never have begun, he thought. Only five years before, the shepherd had had the courage to explore the cave he found while seeking his lost goat in a storm.

With the war at an end and the Middle East in an uproar over the division of Palestine, the country was ripe for the scandalous treatment of such a remarkable find – earthenware jars, many broken but as many as eight intact, containing ancient leather scrolls wrapped in linen.

"Just think of it," Sebastian muttered more to himself than Zayed as he thought things through. "A lone shepherd boy found the cave, returned with his friends and opened one of the sealed jars, and one of the Dead Sea scrolls saw the light of day for the first time in nearly 2,000 years!

"True," he argued with himself. "Things weren't handled well at all there at the beginning. Scrolls were taken, sold to a Sheik, then to a shopkeeper … So much mishandling! Who knows what has been lost!"

He was pacing, muttering to himself, Zayed watching with dismay and distrust.

"And the treasure! No one knows, no one knows! As much as 65 tons of silver and 25 tons of gold and priceless relics … where? We may never know…"

His mind was working overtime, thinking, perhaps this was the first break he was going to get. "But the Ecole Biblique! Dastardly …"

That made up his mind. Impulsively he asked, "Would you consider working for me?"

Zayed, too, was looking for a break, but he wanted to work for a reputable person; he didn't want to be treated like most Bedouin had since the discovery. He tried to check out Sebastian's credentials as best he knew how.

"What are you doing here?" Zayed asked.

Sebastian thought it was time to level with this smart child who seemed so interested in the history of this place.

"For five years, the Ecole Biblique has been in charge of the scrolls," Sebastian started explaining his frustration, "but they refuse to let anyone see the originals or have access to their translations. They only release Biblically insignificant scrolls."

Zayed listened excitedly, thinking perhaps he had found someone in whom he could confide. He interrupted, "I know! That's why they fired me; I want to learn more, to know more."

Sebastian nodded, enthused by his guest's agreement. Sebastian continued, "I want to get copies of ALL of the scrolls and then release them to a museum in California for study and publication to the world."

Then Sebastian leaned closer to Zayed and whispered confidentially, "If things work out, I could get you a visa so you could study under the scholars at the Huntington Museum and learn all about these scrolls … that is if you agree that all the translations should be shared with the rest of the world."

Zayed was beaming. "Absolutely! Yes I do."

Sebastian was enthralled. "When can you start?"

"Immediately. And, as I am working for you, I have two surprises for you that the Ecole Biblique does not know about."

Sebastian leaned forward, clearly interested, he was so excited he didn't know what to do.

"My cousin is the photographer for the Ecole Biblique; he has photographs of every scroll recovered. He will give them to me when he has photographed all the scrolls."

Sebastian was ecstatic, more than he could have dreamed of. "Ohhhh! A miracle! And the other surprise?"

"I will have to show you. Meet me here before dawn tomorrow morning."

THE LAST SCROLL

DEAD SEA MOUNTAINS - THE NEXT DAY

Sebastian was so excited he couldn't sleep. He was up and dressed well before dawn and walked over to the central kitchen area of his expedition to make his morning cup of tea. Zayed was waiting for him at the camp.

As Sebastian sauntered over to Zayed, dressed in his desert whites, Zayed exclaimed, "We must hurry, Mr. Sebastian!"

Sebastian answered in his typical pampered tone. "What? No time for tea? Well I'll be."

Sebastian was way too curious to make any point of his morning "cuppa" so he trotted after Zayed. When he couldn't restrain his curiosity any longer, he had to enquire, "What is this surprise?"

"I found a cave that I didn't tell the French about. There is a Roman soldier there, and tucked into his uniform is a scroll that I haven't touched. I knew if the French got it, they would not tell me what it said."

Sebastian was dressed as if he were going to a tropical tea party, but he doubled his step, easily matching Zayed, exclaiming, "You know, Zayed, God works in mysterious ways. It is almost as if God wanted us to work together, as if he wants the scrolls to be public property, not hidden in some vault in the Vatican."

Sebastian and Zayed climbed an old mountain goat trail, squeezed between some rocks and Zayed stopped suddenly, the entrance just ahead. The morning light of the rising sun shone through an opening to illuminate the chamber. Sebastian was speechless; he nodded and followed the boy.

They squeezed around and over a rock to enter a chamber, dark and dry. Through an opening about 10 o'clock high, light began to fill the chamber. The skeleton of a headless Roman Centurion sat against the far wall. Between his legs, his skull rested inside an ornate helmet with red feather-like material running across the top like a Mohawk and a crest on his face guard of a fish. His fancy ornate chest harness displayed rows of medals, still attached to his skeletal chest.

To his side lay a shield, as tall as a man, made of wood and covered with leather. Lying in the shield was a baton-like stick and a crude knife.

Sebastian gently removed the papyrus scroll and opened it. "Let's sit down, Zayed. I will translate this for you. It is written in Ancient Aramaic."

Sebastian's voice shook with emotion as he read and translated for the boy.

"This scroll is written for me by my Nephew and scribe, Hilal. The soldier you see here is one of the Roman murderers. A Centurion of Centurions, he commanded 100 officers who each commanded 100 men. This captain was the only survivor of a miracle, orchestrated by God that saved us, and hid the location of the scrolls removed from the second Temple just days before the Romans plundered Jerusalem.

"Ten thousand Romans were camped in the valley of Qumran, searching for us. We were surrounded with no escape possible. Only God could help us now.

"As we were about to give ourselves up, a great wall of water rose from the Dead Sea, walked over land to the Roman camp and swept all away into a ravine of raging angry water. They were all lost, save this Roman, who was spared so that I could exact the vengeance for which I had prayed.

"The Teacher of Righteousness and I attest to this true account of this day and to the scrolls of the second Temple.

"My Nephew tells me that many, many years in the future a Bedouin shepherd boy will unearth these scrolls. I don't know how this is possible, but he says the little Bedouin who finds the scrolls will be called Zayed Thanoon, a direct descendant of mine.

"Sworn to be the truth,

"Thanoon, Uncle of Hilal."

Sebastian looked over at Zayed, who was trembling. Concerned for the boy, he asked, "What is it, Zayed? What's the matter?"

It was several seconds before Zayed was able to answer, gasping for air, "My name," he said. "My name."

"What?" Sebastian shouted, more concerned now than ever.

Zayed managed to calm down enough to reply. "My name is Muhammad Zayed Thanoon."

ABOUT THE AUTHOR

A love for adventure as a young boy, travel across the African continent as a young man and a brief stint in Sao Paulo chasing after an elusive dream girl fed into the over-active imagination of Spencer Hawke to produce a plethora of interesting projects. During his travels, he spent many cold desert nights watching Bedouin campfires in the distance while an un-trusty Land Rover left him high and dry, and in that imagination, the tale you just read began to take shape. At home in Oklahoma City, Spencer spends his days with grandson, Devon, already an avid adventurer, and is always working on his next four or five projects …

Made in the USA
San Bernardino, CA
15 January 2017